Revenge in Rio

by

Samantha Darling

Revenge in Rio

ISBN: 978-1-940744-78-0

Edited by Leigh Lamb

Cover Art by Fantasia Frog Designs

Published in the United States of America by Beachwalk Press, Incorporated

www.beachwalkpress.com

Dedication

For my Nan, who loves romance stories just as much as me..

Acknowledgements

Several amazing people have made this book possible, from the very beginning, to the very end—you know who you are.

A special thank you has to go out to the wonderful editors at Beachwalk Press, Leigh and Pamela, who worked their literacy magic to scrub my rough stone into a beaming diamond!

Also an extra special thank you has to go to my dear friends, Christy and Annie. I couldn't have done this without you both. You are two very special ladies. X

Chapter 1

Luca Venancio's cellphone vibrated against the glass table, interrupting the business negotiations taking place in the boardroom of his New York office. Light flooded the space through the huge, floor-to-ceiling windows, and sharp rays of morning sun bounced on and off of the table. The strong light emphasized several pieces of expensive artwork on the walls. The room's opulence, with its fiercely modern lines, complimented his lifestyle one hundred percent.

The private detective's name flashed on the screen and Luca pressed the receive button, holding the phone to his ear. "Yes, Steve?"

"Luca, you got a minute?"

"Sure."

He covered the phone with his hand and said, "Gentlemen, excuse me," while exiting the boardroom. He certainly didn't want an audience for the rest of the phone call.

He was playing with fire by walking out on important negotiations worth billions, but he had to take this call. Steve wasn't due to contact him until his usual

Friday morning arrangement, and was three days early. Luca knew something had to be wrong.

He retreated to the privacy of his office and sat down, resting his elbows on the antique desk, which somehow seemed out of place in his clinical, contemporary office suite. “Okay. I’m listening.” His heart pounded hard in his chest and uneasiness began to creep its way through his body, inch by inch.

Was she okay? Was she hurt? His mind raced with hundreds of possibilities, each one causing his concern to increase. Not that it should have bothered him. Daniella Venancio had nothing to do with him anymore, and he sometimes found himself questioning why on earth he still checked her wellbeing. Did it ease his pain? Comfort his broken heart? No. Honestly, it often left him even more bitter about their previous relationship, but he still continued with the weekly arrangement, because he just had to know for himself.

The detective coughed and cleared his throat before he spoke. “Daniella is attending a funeral tomorrow.”

The awkward, edgy feeling slowly melted away, and Luca’s muscles loosened one by one. He now knew she was still alive. For a second, he didn’t care about anything else, as long as he knew Daniella was all right, that was all that mattered. As much as he despised her for what she'd done to him, he would never in a thousand dreams wish her dead.

"Whose funeral?"

"Miguel's." The investigator's voice was assured and confident.

Luca swallowed hard, and a sudden pain gripped his throat. "When? How?"

"Your brother was found in the early hours of this morning. I don't know the exact details, but it looks gang related…"

Luca listened carefully, taking in the facts of what had happened. A dangerous concoction of alcohol, drugs, and street gangs. His body was numbed by the sad news. A life taken too young. His brother had lived a risky life; the shanty, or *favela*, was a perilous place. Luca had been in Miguel's position himself many years ago, and he'd tried several times to help his younger brother start afresh, but Miguel wouldn't accept Luca's assistance. There had been animosity between the brothers since they were children and, more recently, Daniella had come between them.

"How is Daniella?" The question rolled off his tongue before he could stop it. Usually when he received

Steve's phone calls each Friday, he didn't ask questions. The detective would merely state that Daniella was still in the same location and doing 'okay'. When he'd hired Steve, Luca had informed him that he didn't want to know any details—he simply wanted to know she was alive and well. He couldn't…he *wouldn't* let himself get sucked into an emotional mess by asking questions. Love made people weak, the complete opposite of him. Luca would never let himself be trapped by any woman ever again.

The detective cleared his throat again, his apparent confidence diminishing as hesitation crept in and lingered on the telephone line between the two men.

"It's fine," he reassured the detective who was about to break their one and only rule. "Tell me."

"She's looked better, Luca. She looks weak and has attended a clinic several times recently. The nurse wouldn't tell me what for."

Luca shut his eyes tightly, immediately regretting his question.

He didn't need to interrogate Steve about the arrangements, he knew exactly where the funeral would be taking place.

"I'll be in touch." Luca ended the call and sat back

on the soft leather. He rubbed his temples with firm fingers, trying to push away the approaching headache.

He sighed and threw his cellphone onto the desk with a thud and reached into the drink cabinet for the fine Scotch whiskey he kept handy. He took a long and generous swig from the bottle, allowing the peaty taste to numb his throat. Once the burning sensation had faded and he'd managed to process the conversation, Luca poured a second measure into a crystal tumbler. The whiskey rolled around his tongue and he appreciated the expensive quality this time.

Luca's head ached and he closed his eyes, remembering the only girl he had ever loved, an emotion he had kept hidden for a long time. He was never short of female company, but none of them meant anything to him except her.

Opening up his laptop, he typed a password into a protected document, revealing several photographs of Daniella. He ran his thumb over the screen, recalling the touch of her skin, how it once had radiated heat and burned with such desire for him. Just him.

He should have been concentrating on the sad news of the death of his brother, yet his mind wandered to his past flame, his ex-fiancée. Luca closed his eyes again and saw the first time he'd met her. He'd watched her shopping bags split, a cascade of fresh oranges rolling across the busy road. Cars sounded their horns and bikes rang their bells as she'd stepped out to reach for the fallen goods. Luca rushed behind her, whisking her away from the speeding lorry and into the safety of his arms. Inches away, the dozen oranges were pounded into the tarmac.

"*Você está bem*?" Are you okay, he'd asked, her body shaking against his.

She'd looked up at him, her long eyelashes framing her striking emerald eyes. His arms enclosed around her midriff, holding her body close. Her flyaway mahogany curls had come loose from the ponytail banding and illuminated her face. She'd appeared stumped for words, but managed to mutter a sincere, "Thank you."

"You're welcome." He'd met her gaze and sensed an instant connection. He'd felt intoxicated. He'd wanted to know more about her and had needed to see her again. The rest was history. Literally.

He silently cursed, closing the laptop. He needed to pay his respects to his brother even if he wasn't welcome. His heartbeat quickened when he thought about Daniella. It pained him to admit it, but she still had an uncontrollable effect on him. Pushing the intercom, he told his secretary to reschedule his earlier meeting.

He was going back to Rio.

* * * *

Luca had tried to sleep through the flight; anything to lessen the overwhelming images of his brother and Daniella. He landed at Rio's Galeaos International Airport the following morning, slid comfortably into the chauffeur-driven Bentley awaiting his arrival, and headed straight to the cemetery. He'd washed and changed into a fresh tailored suit whilst onboard his private jet and felt ready to take on the day.

There were many cemeteries around Rio, but he was sure Miguel would be buried beside his parents and fellow gang brothers. It was the nearest cemetery to the *favela* of Rocinha and was the cheapest service available.

He hadn't had the best relationship with his brother, but knew paying his respects was the honorable thing to do. There were at least thirty men present, and he knew they were gang brothers, linked by the matching tattoos on their necks and arms. Lifting a hand to his neck, he traced his fingers over a raised scar left by laser removal surgery. Another reminder of his previous wayward life.

He pulled his shirt collar up a fraction higher.

The rain pelted the roof of the car as he scanned the graveyard, searching for Daniella with the burning desire that slowly overtook him. There was no sign of her and the service was nearing the end. Taking a deep breath, he reminded himself why he was there—for his brother's funeral and to have his revenge on her. Now was the time. He wouldn't have dared whilst his brother was alive–he'd had to reluctantly honor their marriage, but now he could play any game he liked. He was determined to make her fall for him again, and he would have her in the palm of his hand within days. He would make her experience the pain, the physical and emotional agony his heart had felt for weeks. Months. Even to this day. He had ached so much he hadn't been sure if he would ever feel normal again. Over time, he'd managed to suppress the whirlwind of emotions and vowed he would never love again.

A small figure appeared on the edge of the crowd, and he leaned forward and squinted, trying to focus through the constant rain.

It was her. The petite frame, the shapely curve of her hips, and the damp curls loosely dancing in the storm's breeze were so familiar to him. His heart started to pound hard and his palms were clammy. He reached for the handle, threw open the door, and stepped out into the tropical downpour. The last five years vanished in an instant, here she was now in front of him, and he wasn't going to let her go.

"Daniella," he yelled. He didn't care if Miguel's gang saw him. "Daniella," he shouted again, louder this time.

She turned to face him. Shock was evident on her face, and she started to back away, taking steps out into the rain. The shelter from the large Avores tree no longer protected her from the torrential weather. He sprinted to catch up to her as she was clearly trying her best to outdo him, but heels and the rain slowed her flight and she was no match for his athletic fitness. Reaching out, he grabbed for her, and his hand closed tightly around her fragile wrist. The rapid beating of her pulse radiated through his fingers and mixed with his own. She stopped, but tried to pull away from his grip.

Luca spoke, still firmly holding on to her wrist. "Daniella, what…why did you run?"

The rain pelted down, tumbling down their cheeks and soaking their clothes. Fat rain droplets hit against Daniella's bronzed skin and slid down the v-neck of her dress and he couldn't drag his gaze away.

Focus!

He cursed. He had wanted to see her to get the answers he needed, but his brain had switched a gear and her beauty was distracting him from his purpose. Steve had been right, she had looked better. She was a shadow of her former self. Yet her natural beauty was still visible through the gauntness of her cheeks.

He had come there with a plan and he was determined to stick to it. He could not let himself be swayed by this woman.

She tried to pull away and he tightened his hold.

"You said you would never come back," she shouted at him through the deafening rain.

"Well, surprise." He gloated, unable to help himself.

She took a deep breath before she answered. "You're not meant to be here. How did you find out?" Her voice was panicked and her arm trembled.

"Why do you underestimate me? You weren't going to tell me that my own brother is dead?" he said, trying to pull her closer.

Taking a steadying breath, he reminded himself that he needed Daniella on his side for his plan to work.

"Let go of me please," she begged, using all of her weight to pull away from him.

"We need to talk." He composed himself.

"No, you need to leave." She tugged away from his hold and urgency tainted her words.

Luca kept his grip on her wrist, but lessened the pressure. He caught her look away toward the group of men and the approaching taxi slowly making its way up the dirt track entrance. Her bottom lip trembled, as if she was ready to burst into floods of tears. Dark curls tumbled around her face and shoulders in the breeze, but it didn't hide the sunken hollows underneath her once expressive eyes. Nor did it hide the fading bruises across her jaw. She pulled the baggy cardigan tightly around her body.

"Who did this to you?" He gasped, reaching to push her hair aside.

She flinched, recoiling from his gentle touch.

"You don't need to be scared of me. You know I would never hurt you," he lied, knowing his plan was to intentionally hurt her. Maybe not physically, but emotionally. It was equally as excruciating as physical pain, if not worse. He knew from first-hand experience. Guilt now riddled him as he watched the woman before him wince. How the hell was he going to see through his revenge? It was impossible. She looked ill and weak, and he couldn't damage her further. Could he?

"I was just clumsy. It's nothing."

"It doesn't look like nothing."

"Please, Luca, just go. I'm begging you, just leave here. Leave Rio. Leave Brazil," she pleaded with him, still avoiding his eyes.

"Let me take you home. My car is over there." He pointed through the trees.

"No."

"*Ei, Venancio! Você não é bem-vindo aqui!*"

Luca turned to face the group of men yelling at him, telling him he was not welcome. He knew they would be armed and ready for a fight.

Signaling to his chauffeur, the Bentley pulled up beside him within seconds.

"Get in," he ordered, opening the door nearest to Daniella and tugging firmly on her wrist.

She looked back toward the group of men who were now moving closer, and then back to the open car door. The rain still pelted down hard, and both of them were soaked.

"I can't," she cried, her eyes fixed on the

approaching group.

"Get in," he barked, giving her a subtle but firm push toward the car.

Taking one last look at the group of men and her husband's grave, Daniella sucked in a deep breath and slid into the car. Luca was beside her within seconds and they were whisked away down the dirt track, heading toward the smoldering heat of Rocinha.

* * * *

Venturing deeper into Rocinha, makeshift houses piled upon one another as if deliberately balanced. The contrast was apparent, yet the juxtaposition of the *favela* and the city blended effortlessly to encompass the luxurious skyscrapers and million dollar homes around Rio's bay and mountainside.

A painful silence lingered between Daniela and Luca, covered only by the purring of the car's engine. His mind was a blur; he couldn't understand why she had run from him. She had been scared, terrified in fact. He'd felt her pulse racing uncontrollably when he had gripped her arm. Frowning, he ran a hand through his slick, wet hair. Raindrops trickled from the ends of his hair, his nose, and his eyelashes, landing on the car's leather interior.

"Daniella, I need answers." Luca finally broke the icy atmosphere. "Why didn't you care enough to tell me about Miguel?"

He turned toward her and she recoiled, pushing herself against the car door, but still held her cardigan tightly across her body.

"I will get out here," she said, reaching for the door handle.

"No, keep driving," he ordered, glaring at the chauffeur and pressing the central lock button.

Although he hadn't been back to the house, he clearly remembered where his brother had lived. It had been his parents' home and he had grown up there. He would never forget the decrepit building that had desperately needed restoring. Paint had chipped and flaked off of the dreary walls, and the rooms were so small they felt claustrophobic. He had spent many nights sitting on the roof listening to faint arguments between his parents, whilst he dreamed of a better life.

"You don't think I at least deserve an explanation? Some minor clarification as to why you just left me in the dark?" Luca stared at her intently and she opened and then quickly closed her mouth again, biting down on her bottom lip until it darkened to a deeper tone of pink.

He kept his eyes on her, not even blinking, as he looked her up and down. She was a shadow of the vibrant girl he remembered; the Daniella he had known five years ago. Sitting beside him now she was scared, the fear was wild in her eyes, and she was clearly malnourished, evident from the black sack of a dress, which hung off her delicate frame.

"When did you last eat something?" It was more of a demand than a question.

"Excuse me?" He finally had her attention.

"You heard me. When did you last eat something?"

"That's none of your business." She pulled the cardigan tighter around her midriff and turned away from him.

"I'm concerned. You look ill."

"Well, I'm not. I'm…I'm…" He watched as she stumbled for her words. "I'm just grieving, okay?"

Fair enough, she may have been grieving for the last twenty-four hours. It was bound to have been a grueling short space of time for her to comprehend Miguel's death and have the customary quick funeral. But what about before Miguel's death? The circles under her eyes and fading blue marks across her jaw were old; her skin and hair were dull and lifeless and told a story.

They sat in silence as the chauffeur strategically maneuvered the Bentley through the *favela*'s never-ending maze of winding roads, passing makeshift house upon house, small street markets, and gangs on each corner. Luca's eyes fixed on the house in front of them when the car eased to a halt a few meters away from their destination, and he recognized it instantly as his childhood home.

Reaching for the door, Daniella pulled on it a couple of times before he pressed the central locking release.

She looked over her shoulder and whispered, "You really have to go now."

He had given in far too easily years ago, this time he was a different man; a man who always got what he wanted, however cruel and ruthless he had to be. He had to remember that. Love had left him weak and feeble. It had taken time to gather himself and learn to never let emotions take over. Work was his haven, a place for him to focus and throw himself and his energy into. He would prove to Daniella that she had made the wrong choice.

Placing a hand on her shoulder, Luca's fingers brushed against her dark curls and the nape of her neck.

"I'm not going anywhere this time." He leaned closer, his gaze fixed on her mouth. "I've come for something and I intend to get it."

Chapter 2

Daniella could feel the prying gaze of the neighbors as she reached into her purse for the keys. Ladies and children standing on their doorsteps, whispering and pointing; men conversing on the pathway, some with weapons obviously on display for a reaction.

Her hand trembled as she fumbled to position the key in the lock before she dropped them on the cement step outside of the front door.

"Damn," she cursed.

"Here," offered Luca, gently taking the keys from her quivering hand. "Let me."

"You really shouldn't be here," she whispered, holding her head low and avoiding the intense stares. She knew Miguel's cronies would be there soon and Luca's life was in potential danger. Why wouldn't he just leave?

He pushed open the wooden door and extended his arm. "After you."

She looked at his face for a brief moment, avoiding his eyes. She couldn't allow herself to fall into those dark, enticing pools. Silently, she pleaded with him to leave. If only he knew how much danger he was putting himself in, how many wounds he was opening up. Yet, selfishly, she'd never been so happy to see him. He raised his eyebrows and nodded toward the entrance, his arm still holding the door open wide.

Daniella took a deep breath and hurried into the small place she'd called home for the last five years, its dark and oppressive feel ironically welcoming her. For now, it provided a haven away from the gossips and unwanted looks, but she wanted nothing more than to leave it behind. She fastened the lock behind Luca and rested her hands and forehead on the door to steady herself. She was thankful for the solid support against her weary body as the tiredness of her pregnancy washed over her.

She was coming up to seven months and was sure she was meant to be feeling the 'healthy glow' people always spoke about. Her pregnancy barely showed through her baggy clothes. She knew full well she needed to take better care of herself and her baby, but how? Miguel had controlled their finances, usually resulting with him spending the money on his illegal habits. The child, the 'accident' as he had so often said, had meant nothing to him. The bruises she wore reflected that, and she knew the fact her baby still lived was a miracle. She reassured herself that Miguel was gone—forever—and they were both now safe.

"Are you okay?"

She had to pull herself together, otherwise Luca would start asking questions. More questions than she was prepared for.

"I'm fine. It's just been a long…day. I can't believe that you are here." She turned to stand in front of him and hesitated before she spoke. She didn't want to spill too much information.

"In the flesh. Why don't you rest? I can prepare you something to eat." Luca pulled out a chair for her, its legs scraping against the wooden floor.

Why was he being so friendly, so cooperative?

Instantly her guard went up. 'Friendly' was something she hadn't encountered for some time. It filled her with anxiety and apprehension, and her stomach somersaulted with a swarm of nervous butterflies.

Luca's gaze was fixed on her and appeared to be taking in every inch. She felt vulnerable, exposed, as if she was under a magnifying glass for close scrutiny. Could he see her bump? She panicked and fidgeted to draw his attention away from her body. She ran her fingers through her wet curls and pulled them forward slightly to hide the recent bruise across her jaw. Another product of Miguel's foul temper.

"Sit down," he said.

His voice made her feel even woozier than pregnancy did. He had an American twang, yet there was no denying that his rich, Brazilian accent had never left him as it flavored his words. Daniella didn't want to respond to his orders, but she was exhausted and her body betrayed her by taking steps into the kitchenette lounge and sitting down in front of him. She was thankful to finally have the weight off her throbbing, aching feet. She shuffled in the chair and rearranged her cardigan so it covered her small bump.

Luca looked around the room.

A day hadn't passed by where she hadn't thought of him and how her life could have been so different. She'd prayed every day that he was safe and well, a million miles away from the danger and memories Rio held for him. At night, she would curl into herself and wish his arms were embracing her instead of her own.

Now, he stood before her and she resisted with all her might the urge to confess how much she loved him and wanted him. She'd always wanted him…just him.

No. She couldn't. Luca couldn't know of the past. She couldn't let him know what had happened, what she'd done for him. Time had passed and there was no point bringing things up to just cause further heartache.

Her eyes were on the level with his chest, and she watched him breathe for a few moments. Daniella lifted her head warily and absorbed every detail of his towering physique. She recalled how powerful he was, how well defined his muscles were, and how she'd once traced her fingers over them. She let her gaze linger on his sculptured jaw and mouth, his closely shaven face, and his slightly crooked nose.

Smaller droplets of rain continued to drip from his sleek, black locks. She resisted the urge to run her fingers through his hair and instead she stood and reached to a nearby cupboard.

"Here." She handed him a small towel and took one for herself.

He took it from her hands, grazing her skin. "Thanks."

Daniella glanced at her arm where he'd briefly brushed against her. An electric sensation radiated throughout her body, and she longed for his touch further. He rubbed the towel over his face and hair, leaving it more relaxed and natural.

As much as she wanted to, she couldn't bring herself to look into his eyes, knowing once she did she would be trapped. Part of her resented him for leaving, although she knew it was completely irrational to feel that way. Luca had left, blissfully unaware of the truth. She had made him leave.

Standing inches from Luca, so handsome and striking, she was now lost for words. She opened and closed her mouth several times in an attempt to string sentences together, but no sound escaped.

How could he stand there so effortlessly, so cool? Did he no longer have feelings for her? Was he now married with children? *Of course he is.* He wasn't going to wait around for a girl he couldn't have anymore, especially after the way she'd treated him. Daniella started to panic and regretted taking his offer of a lift home, not that she'd had much choice in the matter.

Time seemed to slow and pass by in milliseconds as the awkward silence between them stretched on. She could hear the hustle and bustle going on outside on the *favela* streets; it was amplified against their stillness. An assortment of noises, including Brazilian beats, car horns, and chattering, could be heard through the thin walls of the home.

Luca leaned in slightly and lifted his hand to her chin.

"Has a doctor taken a look at your face?" he asked, and stretched forward to inspect the bruise more closely.

"No. It's nothing. I don't need to see a doctor."

"It doesn't look like nothing. You can talk to me."

If only he knew.

"Please, I'm fine," she begged, holding up a hand to signal an end to his questions.

His eyebrows drew together and an inquisitive look crossed his face.

Please, no more questions.

She watched him back away; his handsome face relaxed and untroubled as the frown lines faded one by one. Her gaze remained on him as he walked about her 'house in one room' with hands thrust deep into his trouser pockets, as if he was retracing his childhood steps. She hated the way he commanded the space. It made her feel so insignificant, more than she already did. His height, his poise, his aura, everything seemed to tower over her pointless life.

No, she cursed herself again shutting her eyes

tightly. She couldn't think that way anymore. She had a reason to live now, and she had to be strong for her baby. Daniella rested her hand on her tummy as if greeting her growing child before quickly removing it, remembering she was in Luca's company. She certainly didn't want him knowing about her pregnancy. She was thankful for the loose fitting dress and cardigan that covered the small, still telltale evidence of a baby bump.

Plucking all of the confidence she could muster within, she folded her arms across her chest. "Why are you here, Luca? What do you want?"

As Luca replaced an ornament he'd picked up to inspect, Daniella bit her bottom lip. She wondered how he'd known about Miguel, but then remembered his statement: *Don't underestimate me.*

"So, you gave up everything we had…for this? Did he treat you well? Love you?" His eyebrows rose.

His gaze returned to her, traveling up and down her body as if searching for answers. She couldn't answer him. His look was so intense, she started to feel as if she was on fire; heat filled her belly and spread up within her. Her chest, her neck, her cheeks, she could feel herself start to flush.

Deep down inside, she knew the desire she'd had

for him years ago was still there. It would always be there. But now, a thousand suppressed emotions had started to re-surface within her and she wasn't sure how to handle them. She'd been forced to leave Luca, but she could never be made to stop loving him. Needing to break away from his connection, she walked to the kitchen sink, poured a glass of water, and took a couple of long gulps, hoping it would put out the heat consuming her.

"Why am I here?" He massaged his chin with his thumb and index finger. He had pronounced each word slowly and accurately, his calm tone matching his leisurely, confident steps toward her. "Remember, Rio and this place were my home too. Once." He continued to inspect photographs and knickknacks, as if placing ownership on the room. "Obviously, I wanted to attend my little brother's funeral. When I heard the sad news, I wanted to pay my respects, as you can only imagine, I'm sure. We may not have been close, but he was of my blood." He glanced at her over his shoulder.

Daniella bit her tongue. He was right. It had been his home, long before it was hers. He had been born in this house and had spent his childhood here, along with Miguel and their parents.

She watched him cast a gaze about the room and prayed to God he wouldn't see her earlier packed escape suitcase tucked beside the sofa. She had no idea where she was going to go, with such little money in her pocket it would be impossible for her to go far. Her birthplace of New York was out of the question, for now. She knew he would try and stop her leaving, and God forbid, if he knew about the baby, he wouldn't let her out of his sight. Family and obligation was important to him, it always had been. Daniella had never understood why he had tried so hard to hold on to family connections, on to his younger brother. The endless times Luca had tried to help Miguel out of trouble, to just be pushed away repeatedly had broken Daniella's heart. Having both his parents and now his brother deceased, she and the child were pretty much all he had left to call family. They were the same; alone in the world with no family around them, apart from each other.

"How did you find out about Miguel?"

"That doesn't matter."

"Your brother was involved in a lot of terrible things, Luca." There was a long pause, and she took another deep breath, composed her wavering voice, and continued. "This…well, this was just a matter of time.

You, of all people, shouldn't be surprised by it. You've paid your respects, you can leave now."

"Hmm, I could, but like I said, I've also come for something else."

The ceiling was low and very nearly touching Luca's head; he looked completely out of place. She glanced over his designer, tailor-made attire and imagined him living amongst opulence and luxury of every kind. He didn't look like a *favela* slum boy. She imagined him owning huge, elegantly decorated dining rooms and extravagant four-poster beds, not the four-walled home she resided in.

She suddenly became aware that his gaze was skimming across her tummy. She couldn't let him find out about her baby. She wanted…no, she needed to get away from the Venancios and start a new life. Completely. She had to leave all of the heartbreak behind her. She would not allow Luca to take control of her life or that of the child she carried.

"What do you think you're doing?" Daniella snapped as he opened her kitchen cupboards.

"You look like a ghost. I understand you're a grieving widow, but you have to eat something. Miguel would want—"

"Miguel would want what?" she interrupted, spitting the words at him with venom.

She looked up and he finally trapped her with his gaze. Those rich, mahogany-colored eyes.

Oh damn, she cursed silently.

She couldn't blink; it was as if he had hypnotized her. Her arms and legs felt like dead weights and her heart was pounding. He reached forward and brushed one of her curls aside. Without hesitation, she let him follow through with his soft and gentle action. Her tense muscles relaxed one by one as warmth and serenity stole over her. His fingers lightly grazed against her skin again, and the small hairs all over her body stood on end and practically begged for further attention. It was a type of touch she'd never received, nor wanted to receive, from Miguel. Daniella shivered as Luca's hands left her body, and for a brief moment she longed for his touch to last forever.

"Ah, so you can see me after all," he drawled, smugness in his tone.

Her stare back at him was confident, although her knees were shaking like a timid child. She reminded herself of her current predicament and that she must forget about their history. There was no point torturing herself with the ifs, buts, or maybes. It was a lifetime ago. This was now, and right now she needed to focus on her baby.

"I merely meant Miguel would want to see you live your life, happy and healthy, wouldn't he?" She sensed a hint of sensitivity in his voice.

Unable to hold back she let out a cold, sarcastic laugh. Luca couldn't have been further from the truth if he'd tried. She desperately wanted to tell him how his brother had treated her and that she had prayed for this day. The warmth and calmness disappeared instantly as her self-preservation and self-protection kicked in.

"Something's funny?" Luca quizzed her.

Daniella tried to hold her temper. Control was so important; it was all she had left now and she had to hold onto it. This was her opportunity for a fresh start. Alone. She simply needed to 'act' the grieving widow for a few more minutes and then Luca would be gone.

"Are you planning on going somewhere?" He nodded toward the case tucked away neatly beside the sofa.

Damn! He'd spotted the suitcase, which she now wished she'd taken more care to hide.

"I was thinking of visiting a friend," she lied and

shrugged.

"I see. Well, I will give you a ride."

"No, it's fine. I can make my own way."

He leaned against the kitchen side and looked at her with his arms folded across his broad chest. The earlier downpour had left them both soaked, and his wet shirt clung to his muscular chest. She swallowed against the dryness in her throat, unable to look away.

"Why don't you just tell me where you're going? I want to be able to look out for you now that—"

"Now that what? Now that I'm alone?" She blinked at him as the nerves took hold once again.

"Yes. I want to support you. You're still my family, and this is an extremely difficult time for you. You said so yourself."

* * * *

Luca leaned against the kitchen counter and watched Daniella fidget in front of him.

"I don't have to report my movements to anybody now." The words, laced with venom, flew from her lips.

Why she was so defensive? Yes, she had the right to be upset, to cry, to scream even, to mourn her late husband, but this was different. She had a pained, tormented look in her eyes; the youthful, glowing personality he'd fallen in love with years ago had gone. Had living with his brother been so awful?

Daniella's words were cut short as she doubled over and cried out in pain. Clutching her stomach, she stumbled, trying to grab on to the kitchen bench, but missed. He moved across the room and held her.

"What is it, what's wrong?" he asked, holding on to her tightly.

Tears spilled over and ran down her gaunt cheeks. She turned her head into his chest and the tears wet his shirt further. She tried to speak, but her words were swallowed by another agonized cry. Her nails dug into the material, reaching his skin. She was holding on to him as if her life depended on it.

"We need to get you to a hospital," he insisted.

"No," she cried. "I'll be–"

"That's enough. I'm taking you to a hospital," he ordered.

He scooped her up and held her tightly against him as he quickly made his way back to the car.

Whispers surrounded them and the peering eyes as the voyeurs scooted around the street to get a closer look. Gently, he laid Daniella across the back seat of the Bentley and climbed in next to her as he barked their destination at the chauffeur.

Was she sick? Did she have an illness? A condition? Was she starving herself because of Miguel's sudden death? His head reeled with possibilities as to why she was doubled over in agony next to him.

"Tell me what's wrong, Daniella. I can't help you if you don't tell me," he begged her, taking hold of her free hand and squeezing it.

His throat tightened as he looked upon her and the pain that appeared to be taking hold of her. As much as he had taught himself to hate her over the years, he now felt the deep primitive connection with her. It had always been there. The hurt she'd caused him to carry for the last five years instantly vanished. She bit down hard on her quivering lip and ignored his question.

The car's wheels screeched through the gravel as they sped away. Within seconds they were racing away from the *favela* streets.

Chapter 3

"You're pregnant?" Luca shouted. "You knew? Why didn't you tell me?"

He raked one hand though his hair and the other remained positioned on his hip. He paced the length of the hospital suite and back, his intense stare not leaving the ultrasound screen, which now revealed a small black-and-white flickering image of a tiny baby.

A baby. A baby. A baby. He repeated the two words over in his head, trying to make sense.

Shit. What had he gotten himself into? Planning to take revenge on Daniella proposed to be a piece of cake, but not with an innocent child in the equation. Damn it!

"Why would I? It isn't your concern," she snapped.

She kept her gaze firmly on the female doctor who was dressed in a typical starchy, white coat.

"How? How is this even possible, there is nothing of you! You are skin and bones. If you were pregnant I would have seen…"

Of course he knew how it had happened.

"Mr. Venancio, if you insist on staying, you really do need to calm down." The doctor's soothing voice silenced him. She looked back at Daniella and smiled. "Yes, you look approximately twenty-seven weeks, just coming up to the seventh month," said the doctor as she rolled the ultrasound probe over Daniella's visible, but petite, bump.

"Is my baby okay?" she asked.

Daniella tilted her head to watch the tiny baby almost waving from the screen. Luca searched her face. It was as if the screen's presentation had spellbound her. The hostility had melted away and revealed a glimmer of hope, adoration for the tiny baby.

She didn't even look pregnant! His gaze shifted from her face to her exposed midriff. With the baggy sack of a dress removed and the loose hospital gown exposing her tummy, he could now see she really was pregnant, but he would never have guessed seven months in a million years.

The news of her pregnancy had shocked him. He'd made no allowances for children in his plan of revenge. No allowance at all. He'd planned to entice her to fall back in love with him and then leave her vulnerable and alone, as she'd so easily done to him five years ago. He'd calculated to seduce her, bed her, and get out within a matter of days, not be standing around caring for a newborn several months later. *Damn it!*

"Yes, everything is fine, Mrs. Venancio. I can see ten fingers and ten toes. It sounds as if you were experiencing Braxton Hicks contractions. Try not to worry, these are very common and actually a good sign, believe it or not. Some women can experience mild contractions and others more uncomfortable." The doctor put a reassuring hand on Daniella's arm. "However, you must start looking after yourself. A good diet, some relaxation, and a little TLC from dad also." The doctor winked at Luca.

Daniella's body instantly stiffened and she pulled herself into a sitting position with her back perfectly straight. "No…no…he's not the father." She stumbled over her words and shook her head furiously at the doctor.

"She will be well looked after, Doctor, I will ensure that," he interrupted and took a step closer to the examination couch.

"I would like to check both mother and baby again in a few days if that's okay? Just to be sure," said the doctor as she placed the monitor back in its cradle.

"Of course." His voice echoed off the sterile walls.

"Before I leave, I would also like to take a quick

check on this bruising." The doctor leaned in close and concentrated on Daniella's jaw.

"No, it's okay, Doctor. Thank you, but I'll be fine. I was just clumsy."

"I'd really like to check that—"

"Please. It's fine. Look…" Daniella touched her face and Luca was sure he could see her biting back a flicker of pain as she traced the bluish-colored skin to prove a point to the doctor.

"Okay. Well, we will see how things look in a few days." She wearily contended with her stubborn patient.

"I will be sure to make an appointment before we leave," said Luca, his gaze not leaving Daniella for a second.

"I've said no." She glared at him.

Doctor Menezes crossed the room and looked from Luca to Daniella. "I will leave you both to discuss the details. I'll be just down the hall if you need me." She gave them a warm smile before leaving and clicking the door shut behind her.

"Do you mind?" Daniella held the hospital blanket over her lower half, signaling for him to turn away.

"*Jesus Cristo*, Daniella. *Caramba*! Seven months, why didn't you just tell me earlier instead of running away?"

Luca bit his tongue and turned to face the en-suite. He could hear her rustling about as she removed the gown and stepped into her own damp clothes. Part of him wanted to look over his shoulder and see her slender body in the flesh and not just from recalled memories. He licked his dry lips and forced himself to focus on the terracotta-colored curtains draped in front of him. She'd begged for him to take her to the public hospital in Rocinha, but he'd ignored her plea and insisted on taking her to a private clinic. Offering her the best possible care had not been part of his plan, but it was what had come naturally to him when he'd collected her up into his arms.

"I don't need your help, Luca. I can look after myself."

He turned to face her and saw she was fully dressed. She was still wearing the damp funeral attire…they both were.

"It's not just you that needs looking after now though, is it? You will stay with me. You won't be able to cope with a newborn baby alone. Let me help you. You heard what the doctor said. You need to take things easy."

"I'll be fine. Besides, you wouldn't help. I bet you don't know the first thing about babies."

"I have house staff and I'll interview for a suitable au pair to assist you. You'd have nothing to worry about. Everything would be taken care of. You're carrying a Venancio, Daniella, and my family. I will be a part of this child's life. It's more important than ever now that the father isn't around." He had to say anything to get her on his side.

She shut her eyes and drew a quick breath before opening them to meet Luca's stare. "It's my baby." She challenged him, resting a protective hand on her tummy. "I do not need a stranger looking after my flesh and blood, and I do not need your endless supplies of money flashed around just to make yourself feel better."

"The child needs a father figure, and I can provide that. You know that I'm right." His words were tinged with matter-of-fact arrogance that he knew would irritate her.

It was true he would look after her, but for his benefit. He would have her gone long before the child arrived. He'd keep tabs on her and when the child was born, he'd gain access and take custody of his niece or nephew, fulfilling his clear family obligation to his late brother. She wasn't fit to be a mother.

Luca traced his index finger along his bottom lip as his brain raced. This pregnancy, this baby, could be perfect for more leverage with his revenge against her. He'd break her heart and watch her pine for what she couldn't have. Both him and the child. Just as he had been made to feel. He didn't care for a family, it was the last thing on his agenda now, but if it meant matching the pain he'd been made to suffer by her hand, then so be it.

It hadn't always been this way. He'd once envisioned a two-point-five-child family with a cat or dog, but she'd shattered that vision when she'd left him for his baby brother.

He recognized he was overconfident and egotistical, but he didn't care what people thought. Being those things had earned him the position he was in now, owner of Venancio Mining Company, and amongst the richest people in the world. So what if he was egotistical, he told himself. He remained standing calmly beside the bed with his hands deep in his trouser pockets.

"No," she whispered. "I can't have you in my life. I just can't."

He took a couple of slow paces toward her. "You

can't, or you won't?"

A raw, uncomfortable silence lingered between them as he waited for her to answer.

"Well?"

She sucked in a shaky breath and rolled her bottom lip between her teeth. "Luca, I won't let myself go through any more hurt."

He could hear the fragility in her words, the raw croakiness of her voice. What had happened? Could he really go through with his plan? He swallowed hard. Of course he could.

Remember what she did to you. She left you. For your own brother.

The child wasn't born yet and it wouldn't be affected by his plans. The child would have the best upbringing once he or she was living with him. This was between just him and Daniella for now. He needed to forget about the added extras.

"I'm going home. I'm collecting my things and then I'm leaving Rio. For good."

"And where will you go? With what money?"

"It's none of your business."

"I think you'll find it is my business. I'm the only family this child will have." His eyes flashed to her stomach and then back to her gaze.

“All of your family has passed. You are alone. It’s important this child knows about his or her remaining relatives, their history. I have an obligation now.” He spoke with sarcasm in his voice as if he was gaining enjoyment out of her loneliness. “Or do you consider Miguel’s gang brothers to be the child’s family and support structure? I’m sure they’ll be outstanding role models.”

Her wild, cat-like eyes locked with his and he could see he’d touched a nerve as her body tensed, ready for battle.

“Well, it’s true,” he growled. “You’ll probably have the child signed up and into a gang by the age of five. You can barely look after yourself, let alone a child. Just look at yourself.”

Her pupils dilated as her eyes widened, and her green irises darkened with burning intensity.

“How dare you!” She slapped him hard across the jaw and left a fiery sting. Luca opened his mouth and moved his jaw from side to side a couple of times. She glared at him whilst he massaged his cheek and pride.

“Don’t you patronize me about role models and gang allegiance.” Tears formed at the corners of her eyes. "And don't you dare think you are better than me just because you've had your tattoos removed and run a fancy business. You can't change who you are inside. This—" She waved her hands up and down in his direction. "—is all a show. A cover up. You haven't changed one bit."

Her gaze settled on his scarred skin where his gang affiliated tattoo had once been bared for all to see with….what, pride? It had been a symbol of branding, ownership over him, and a pledged allegiance to a violence-fuelled gang. A gang that he'd led for a period of time in the latter years before he'd fled Rio. As he'd approached his teens, he'd received scant attention from his parents and had been desperate for any sense of belonging, so he considered the local mob as a family. A support network. He couldn't have been further from the truth.

There was nothing supportive about sending a twelve-year-old boy out on to perilous streets armed with a loaded AK-47 and a pocketful of heroin to sell. Once you were in a gang, it was rare you got out…alive.

He pulled his shirt collar tighter around his neck, creating a sense of protection.

"You may not have told me about your dark past,

but your dear, dear brother did. How you used to lead a gang, street fight, sell drugs…you were no better than Miguel."

He stared directly into her eyes. The emerald green pools glowed with a type of energy he didn't remember seeing in her before. It was toxic. Livid.

"Oh yes, Miguel told me about everything. So don't pretend you're high and mighty standing before me now." She didn't blink as she held his stare.

He sucked in a deep breath, but kept his gaze firmly on hers. She was right. He had done all of those things, and he wasn't proud in the slightest. When he'd met her over five years ago, he'd well and truly cleaned himself up and had left his young, wayward life behind him, focusing all of his energy into his given opportunity and now flourishing business. Yes, she'd known where he'd grown up and lived, deep within the Rocinha *favela*, but she didn't know the sordid details of his antics. He'd wanted to keep that tainted part of his life hidden. Forgotten.

That was until Miguel had decided to indulge her.

"You…you have no idea the hell I have been through, Luca, the things I've had to do and been put through. So don't you dare…" She closed her eyes and swallowed. “I will do anything to protect my baby. Anything.”

“I’m not taking ‘no’ for an answer. Everything has changed in the last thirty minutes. There is a new life to consider. You’re staying with me. I will carry you out of here if I have to.”

He’d come to Rio to pay his respects, but to ultimately have his revenge. He needed to remember she wasn’t the naive, innocent little girl who needed protecting. She was a heartbreaker, a family wrecker who needed teaching he reminded himself.

He believed in the old saying ‘an eye for an eye’.

“You can’t simply turn up in my life and after two minutes start giving out your orders, Luca. Your staff may be happy to come running whenever you snap your fingers but I’m not,” she said with her hands on her hips. “I’m not your property.”

You were once mine.

He needed to cool things down if he wanted to see his plan through. He wasn’t in the boardroom now. Ruthless and authoritarian wasn’t going to get him anywhere with her. He turned on his heel and found himself facing the terracotta-colored drapes once again. However much it pained him to be pleasant to her, he had to do it.

He slowly turned back to face her, loosening his tie and top button.

"Okay, I'm sorry. I've gone about this all the wrong way." He opened his palms to her in an apologetic gesture. "Can we start again?"

She fidgeted in front of him, her confident stance softening.

"Listen, you live in a house which needs to be condemned. Hell, it needed condemning when I lived there. You look as if you have not eaten in weeks. You're physically not well. You need stability and caring for. You're pregnant and going to give birth in two months. Let me help you." He reeled off his points one by one using his fingers. He kept his gaze locked with hers as he spoke.

"It's not safe for you to be here. Especially near to the *favela*. I can't believe you're standing here right now. You really need to go."

He saw a flicker of genuine fear in her eyes. Why was she worried?

"You need to leave and just go back to your life."

"I have no idea why you keep saying it's not safe for me here. Is it something to do with Miguel's gang?

So what, I left the gang and broke my allegiance. I am a big boy now, Daniella. I can look after myself."

She shook her head from side to side, mahogany curls danced about her shoulders as she moved.

"Just believe me, please. Go home, Luca." Her words sounded like a plea.

"No." He took hold of her hand and rubbed his thumb across her knuckles soothingly. "Whatever the reason is you fear for me, I don't care. I'm not leaving you and this child. My home here is totally off-the-grid anyway. Nobody would find it even if they had a ton of maps and the latest GPS. The directions are all up here." He lightly tapped his temple with two fingers.

He was nearly there. He could see *yes* on the very tip of her tongue. She just needed one small wave of persuasion and then she would be putty in his hands. Once he had her in his home it would be simple. They would be back on his turf. His territory. His rules.

"I promise I won't let any harm come to either of you."

"It's not us I'm worried about. I wasn't aware you still had a home here?"

After several years of service to one of Rocinha's most dangerous gangs, he'd made a run for it. There was nothing to hold him back, both parents had passed and his brother had sunken deeper into trouble; a trouble that he didn't want to give up. However much he'd wanted to flee Brazil, he'd been unable to part with the property he'd bought and renovated for Daniella and himself, once upon a time.

The sense of freedom when he'd left was indescribable. He tried to match his experience with Daniella's. He was sure she would be craving freedom right now and not his overbearing orders.

"I can look after myself. I promise to give you whatever it is you want–your own space? I travel overseas a lot, so that's not a problem." He shrugged. "You'll have space. Just let me be there for you…you both."

She sucked in a deep breath as if preparing for the next round of battle, but instead she answered quietly. "Fine, but once my baby is born and you see I can manage, we will be leaving."

She pulled her hand away from his light grip and quietly retreated to the en-suite.

* * * *

The chauffeur maneuvered the Bentley through Rio de Janeiro's bustling motorways and narrow side streets, leaving the private clinic in Barra da Tijuca far behind them. They were heading toward the hilly mountain regions where Luca's property was nestled away from civilization. Daniella had shuffled to rest on her right buttock, leaving her back to face him. She hadn't said a word since leaving the clinic and, quite frankly, Luca wasn't sure what to say for once. He closed his eyes and rubbed both eyelids hard with his thumb and index finger. When he opened them, he looked out on to the city that was his birthplace. A place he'd once called home. The cloudless blue skies were turning shades of orange, red, and dusky pink as the evening sun began to set behind the mountaintops and skyscraper roofs.

The chauffeur drove the car further toward the thick, green vegetation following the beaten track and leaving behind the chaotic noise of the city. The panoramic view of the cosmopolitan city below them was breathtaking, Luca had to admit it. The royal azure Ipanema and Copacabana beaches were fully visible in all of their famous glory from this height as the waves lapped at the honey golden sand fringes of the bay. Luca's gaze drifted away from the shorelines and rested upon the unique blend of *favelas* growing upon the stylish city's edge. The shanty homes sprawled along the steep hillsides and around the cusp of the inner city's expansion. In his five-year absence he could see the changes; further *favela* growth spread and ever taller, sleeker, skyscrapers were filling the over-urbanized and crowded city to its limits.

In the distance, he could see the Corcovado Mountain and the Christ the Redeemer statue situated at its peak. The last of the evening sun's rays glittered around the edges of the solid concrete and soapstone artwork, illuminating its beauty and presence for the whole of Rio to adore. Its arms were open wide and ironically, Luca felt as if the statue was welcoming him back to his motherland.

No. He needed to remain focused and remember exactly why he was there and what he had to do. Once it was done, he'd be on the first jet back to New York. Brazil and Rio held nothing for him anymore.

Luca glanced at Daniella. Her eyelashes were lowered and she'd lost the fight to stay awake. Her arms were tightly wrapped around her body, as if to protect herself from the world.

The car pulled off the road and turned right down a dirt track strategically hidden by gatherings of tropical trees either side. His off-the-grid Rio property was just one of his many homes across the globe; small in comparison to the rest of his tasteful collection, though its sentimental value was priceless. His staff immaculately maintained the house and gardens even though he had not visited Rio for five years. He found himself wondering why he'd kept the house and the employees, instead of selling it. Maybe secretly he'd hoped that one day he would have a reason to come back to his birthplace. He didn't want Daniella back and he was never going to give her the property as he'd originally planned. So why had he insisted on keeping it? He pushed the pestering thoughts aside and concentrated on the house before him.

He took in all the details of the estate as the car slowly made its way down the driveway. Nestled away at the bottom of the mile long driveway, large ceramic plant pots filled with an array of vibrant flowers were placed on the steps leading to the front door. The fragrance of the lush trees and *laelias* welcomed him through the open car window, along with the exotic twittering of the native birdlife living nearby.

Whitewashed walls were still as brilliant as the day they had been painted. Huge bay windows draped with elegant curtains were situated on both sides of the heavy wooden front door. He'd insisted on them when the property was being built. He knew how much Daniella loved light and open space, though she had never seen their home. Just days before he'd planned to give her the keys, Miguel had made his move. Daniella had broken his heart and trust as if it was the easiest thing in the world. Women now meant nothing more than a pleasure in his bed. Simple as that.

The chauffeur drove the car through the password protected gates and parked in front of the mansion. Luca stepped out into the muggy evening air and walked to the other side of the car. Daniella didn't move a muscle as he gently picked her up and cradled her close. Deeply asleep, she didn't resist, but rested her head against him and sighed. Luca made his way into the house and up the twisting marble staircase. He laid her down on the master bed—his bed, even if he hadn't slept in it for over five years.

He removed her black dress, which had now completely dried in the intense Rio heat and left her in her underwear. His gaze lingered on her scantily clad body for the briefest of seconds as his attention was again drawn to her delicate frame and neat bump. It was hard to believe there was a child growing inside her. He pulled the sheet over her and encouraged her sleep; she needed to escape, to recharge.

He brushed her hair aside and bent down to kiss her temple. “I’m here now, *querida*, I will look after you both. I promise.”

Were those words part of the plan to seduce her? If so, why had he said them when she was fast asleep? He exited the bedroom and rubbed his eyes hard. He needed to focus on his plan and not let his emotions get the better of him.

“*Olá, Senhor* Venancio.” Maria, one of his longstanding housekeepers, smiled at him, seeming genuinely pleased to see him. “It is good to see you home.”

Luca toyed with Maria’s words. Was he really home? The house was hollow. There was no warmth or body to it, no family portraits, nor children running through the halls. That was a home. He gave the middle-aged lady a courteous smile. “*Olá,* Maria. It’s good to see you too.”

He chatted with her for a few minutes, commented about the hot summer, and asked how her family was doing. Promising to catch up with her tomorrow, he insisted she take the evening off and go home.

He attended to several business calls and emails, ate the salad Maria had prepared for him, and then returned back to the master bedroom. The woman in his bed had not even stirred and remained in the exact same position he'd left her in. He stripped down to his cotton boxer shorts and pulled on a t-shirt. He positioned himself on the sofa opposite the bed. He started to think perhaps he should have put her in one of the guest rooms.

No. He wanted her nearby so he could keep a watchful eye over her. Over them both. She was not leaving his sight this evening or any other until he had succeeded. His plan of revenge and seduction would be put into full throttle tomorrow morning.

Chapter 4

Daniella stirred in the luxury silk sheets and stretched her arms and legs, wriggling her fingers and toes. Blissfully unaware of her whereabouts for the first few waking seconds, she reveled in the calm surrounding her. Then reality came into play. There was no honking of car horns, no loud music vibrating through the walls, and no arguing neighbors. There was nothing, only silence. She opened her eyes and the tropical sun blinded her for a moment. The sun was high and the slanting rays had reached the edge of her bed, touching her bare skin. The bed. The room.

Wondering where she was, she looked around the spacious room, her sight still blurry. The huge floor-to-ceiling windows took up half of the wall space at the far end of the suite. The room was decorated in modern, clean lines, yet there were subtle hints of a traditional feel thrown in amongst the antique wooden furniture, the four-poster bed she was lounging in being one of them. Luca. Yesterday's actions started to replay in her mind. His insistence.

Pulling herself upright, she drew the bedding closer

to her semi-naked body. She looked down at the fabric and frowned. She didn't recall taking her clothes off. In fact, she barely remembered leaving the hospital. She moved her legs over the edge of the tall bed and wrapped the silky smooth material around her body. The polished, wooden floorboards warmed the soles of her feet and creaked slightly when she walked toward the window. She rested her forehead against the bay-shaped window and looked down at a middle-aged man attending to the gardens.

The luscious orchards were thick with vibrant greens, yellows, and purples. Begonias, poppies, and orchids were in full bloom, providing a true Brazilian flavor to the garden. She'd never seen anything quite like it and she instantly wanted to be out in its beauty, allowing the natural energy and tranquility to soothe her. She was going to get dressed and head straight to the garden.

A flush heated her cheeks when she looked down at the sheets that covered her body and realization hit her hard in the stomach. Luca must have undressed her. Anger quickly replaced embarrassment. How dare he! He had no right to do such a thing. She frantically searched the room for her clothes, but couldn't find them. Was this some kind of joke?

Daniella was irritated with herself for being manipulated once again. She wouldn't allow herself to be controlled by another man. He was already monitoring her and she'd been in his company less than twenty-four hours. Too much had happened between her and the Venancios. As much as she had loved…still loved Luca, it would be impossible to stay. It simply wasn't healthy for either of them.

Peeking around the doorframe into an empty hallway, she crept out on tiptoes and slowly made her way toward the staircase at the end of the corridor. Aromas of fresh bread and sweet pastries filled the air and her stomach growled fiercely. She toyed with the idea of finding the kitchen before Luca, not sure whether her stomach, and the baby, could wait any longer. She reached for the intricately carved banister, but stopped when she heard Luca's deep, velvety voice coming from further down the hallway. Backing up, she followed his voice. As she neared him, she could hear he was talking about work, tying up loose ends of a new contract.

She walked into the last room off of the corridor and saw that it opened out onto a large, open planned veranda. More tropical flowers surrounded the balcony and provided a sense of security and privacy. He was sitting at the food-laden table, speaking into the webcam on his laptop.

He turned his head toward her and his gaze traveled up and down her body. A shiver rippled through her, yet she wasn't cold.

"Have your secretaries make contact with your final offering figures and I will be in touch. Good day to you all." He ended the meeting with a nod toward the laptop's inbuilt camera and then shut it.

He stood and walked toward Daniella who was hovering by the doorway.

"*Bom dia.*" He smiled, offering her his hand.

Daniella held the sheet more tightly around her body as she coolly gave him the once-over. He was casually clothed today. Instead of the high-powered, well-fitting Armani suit, he wore tan chinos and a white linen shirt with his sleeves rolled up. The little dark stubble growth added to his relaxed image and good looks. He was the complete opposite to his younger brother whose muse to the alcohol and drugs had left him thin and disheveled. But there was no disputing they were brothers. The dark features and model-like cheekbones were a genetic trait.

She wanted to snap at him, demand to know where her clothes were, and scream that he'd had no right to undress her. Taking a deep breath, she remained calm. "Where are my clothes? Who undressed me? And why was I in your bed?"

Luca's lips curved into a playful smirk, annoying and righteous. "So many questions. Daniella, I left you in plenty. I simply removed your outer clothes due to the heat and for comfort…of course." He took a couple more steps toward her and she could feel the heat radiate from him. "And I wanted you in my room so I could keep an eye on you both, in case you were taken ill again."

Daniella looked up at him for a brief moment before shifting her gaze. She was angry, but part of her was appreciative of him looking after her. She breathed in, slowly regaining her self-control. "Well, you didn't have the right to do any of those things."

Luca looked down and rubbed the back of his neck before he answered. "You don't need to worry, *querida*. I slept on the sofa beside the bed."

Her face filled with warmth, and she was thankful for his gentlemanly behavior—it was something she had not experienced in a long time. She tightened her grip on the sheet and fiddled with the edge, unsure of what to say.

"I believe you slept well?" Luca asked.

Daniella shrugged her shoulders and lied. "I got a couple of hours."

Luca's laughed boomed and echoed around the plush veranda. "You slept for fourteen hours solid and didn't move a muscle."

"I'd like my clothes back please."

"I asked Maria to wash them. I figured after yesterday's weather you would want them freshened up. Have a seat for now." He gestured toward the veranda table. "Have something to eat, you must be hungry."

Daniella desperately wanted to say no to his offer, but her stomach let out another loud growl. She also remembered what the doctor had told her—to start taking care of herself. She was aware of her minimal attire, but hunger pains were taking over and she looked at the feast laid before her.

"Fine, but it's not for your sake."

Luca stepped aside and pulled a seat out for her. Once she had sat, he resumed his position opposite her.

"What would you like? Tea, coffee?" His gaze was fixed on her, but she kept her head bowed.

"Some orange juice will be fine, thank you." She nodded toward the crystal jug beside him.

She watched him pour the freshly squeezed juice until her flute was three-quarters full. She brought the glass to her lips and took a few sips of the pulpy liquid. As she shut her eyes, she enjoyed the fresh, zesty sweetness of the juice as it made her tongue tingle.

She opened her eyes and saw he was watching her intently.

"This is very nice orange juice."

"Homegrown, only the best. Please, help yourself to food."

Daniella was ravenous, it had been a long time since she had eaten a hearty meal. She craned her neck to see what was being offered to her. The table was full of various freshly baked breads, cheeses, jams, butters, yogurts, cereals, and ripe fruits sliced and designed into various patterns and shapes. She wanted to devour everything in front of her, but started by polishing off a couple of slices of sweet almond bread slathered with butter and freshly made strawberry jam.

"How do you feel this morning?"

Swallowing a mouthful, Daniella answered, "I feel fine. I just needed some rest, that's all."

"It's amazing what sleep can do for the mind, body, and soul."

She ached to tell him it was partially the undisturbed sleep partnered with a safe environment and no longer having to fear his abusive brother that had helped her feel ten times healthier as of this morning.

"Hmm." That was all she could muster for now. She couldn't relax under his constant gaze; he watched every bite she took. "Please stop watching me."

Luca's chair screeched as he pushed back against the tiles and she jumped. He threw back the last mouthful of his black coffee and collected his laptop and cellphone.

"Finish your breakfast in peace. Whatever it is you or the baby want, the staff will prepare for you. All you need to do is say."

Daniella looked up at him and shielded her eyes from the sun with her hand.

"Thank you." She meant it.

She could have sworn Luca frowned when she had thanked him, but his expression instantly returned to a smile within a split second, making her wonder if she'd imagined it.

Hell, she could be imagining everything right now

for all she knew. Nothing had seemed real since Luca had appeared at Miguel's funeral. She had prepared herself five years ago, consoled herself that she would never see him again as instructed. Yet, there she was draped in silk sheets, sitting in his Rio stately home, having slept just inches away from him. Her true love.

"When you're finished, there is a guest room at the end of the hallway with an en suite. You'll find my staff has prepared a wardrobe for you. Everything you will need is there for you."

"But I'd like my clothes."

"They will be returned to you, but for now, if you don't like what I am offering for your convenience, fine." He smiled and turned and stepped off of the veranda. "Personally, I am happy with just the bedsheet."

Daniella pulled the material closer around her body, as if his words had caused it to bare her semi-naked body.

Peace and quiet surrounded her; just the faint chirping of tropical birds of paradise could be heard from afar. She relaxed into the wicker chair and let her head fall back. She admitted the long sleep had done her a world of good. Her hands instinctively rested on her tummy, as if greeting her child with a 'good morning', and for a moment she wondered about the sex of her baby. Would she have to buy blues or pinks? Footballs or dollies? She didn't mind, as long as her little one was healthy.

The sun's golden rays washed over her face and recharged her with its vitamin-enriched energy and warmth. Then came another hunger pang, reminding her to eat. Sitting up straight, she tucked into the feast in front of her, no longer worried about spectators.

* * * *

Daniella wanted to protest, but after she'd showered and waited for nearly an hour, she was fed up with wearing a bedsheet or bath towel. She opened the door to the walk-in wardrobe and found several racks of clothes. She estimated there had to be well over a hundred outfits hanging neatly on the rails around the room. Dresses, camisoles, jackets, jeans, shorts, skirts, and trousers in a variety of pretty florals, pastels, bold colors, and patterns. She lifted one of the tags and noticed the garments ranged throughout the different stages of pregnancy; whoever Luca had sent shopping, Daniella had to admit they had good taste. *And expensive taste.*

Just one pair of black silk and lace briefs had a price tag of one hundred and eighty-five dollars. All she wanted was a comfortable pair of jeans and vest top, not Gucci and Prada dresses and heels. She frowned and realized she was going to have to wear Luca's money; it would mean yet another hold he'd have over her. Even though she knew he was nothing like Miguel, she couldn't help but keep her guard up. She removed the tag carefully and stepped into the luxurious lingerie. She had to admit they felt and looked beautiful.

She sighed and plucked a pair of navy loose-fitting linen trousers and a cream spaghetti-strapped top from the midst of the wardrobe. Topping the outfit with a cream, kimono-style, draped cardigan, she shrugged her arms into the material. She was thankful for its coverage of the slowly fading blue-purple marks across her shoulders and arms.

Further arrays of expensive shoes were neatly placed at the other end of the walk-in wardrobe, and she felt spoiled just being given the choice. Daniella quickly decided on a pair of flat silver sandals and fastened the delicate buckles. She then twisted her hair up into a loose chignon and turned to look in the full-length mirror. The dark circles under her eyes had faded a little and her complexion had a slight glow about it. This was the healthiest she'd looked in years, she thought. The clothes were a perfect fit to her frame and actually showed her baby bump. She no longer had to hide it from Luca or protect it from Miguel.

As she left the guest room, she admired the large windows at the far end of the corridor; each of them illuminated the space with the sun's rays dancing across the marble floor and across her feet. She ran her fingers along the hand carved wooden stair banister and traced its intricate details. She took each step slowly, drinking in all of her new surroundings, feeling as if she was a princess in a faraway castle. She wasn't sure how much Luca earned, nor did she really care to know, but she was pretty certain his bank account was fully equipped for years' worth of rainy days if his home was anything to go by.

Once she had reached the last step, she looked left and then right, unsure which way to go. As if by magic, a lady appeared holding a small tray with a glass of cold, fresh orange juice placed in the middle.

Is this Maria?

"*Olà, Senhorita* Venancio. I'm Maria, the housekeeper. Here, drink this. It's full of lots of vitamins." She gave Daniella a sweet smile and ran a fleeting glance over her tummy. "You slept well?"

Clearly Luca had already told his staff about her pregnancy. Maybe this lady was the mystery wardrobe shopper? Though she doubted it. Maria was into her sixties and a little out of touch with fashion. Daniella was sure the mystery shopper was a young woman, most probably one of his many employees.

She nodded shyly. "*Sim*, thank you," she said, taking the glass and bending to look over Maria's shoulder. "I'm looking for Luca…"

"*Sim, sim, Senhor* Venancio is in the gardens working," Maria gushed, taking hold of Daniella's arm.

"If he's working I can see him later. I don't want to disturb him," said Daniella, pulling away from the surprisingly strong older lady.

"No, it is fine. He has told me to fetch you. He wants to see you now." She grinned and tugged her arm. "Come."

Daniella found herself being ushered along by the whirlwind that was Maria, whose sandals loudly clip-clopped against the marble flooring throughout the grand mansion. Maria led her out into the open gardens where tropical fragrances swirled around her and gave her reason to fall back in love with Rio, with Brazil, and forget the bad. The housekeeper patted her arm and then left her side. She squinted and scanned the garden's horizon for Luca. She spotted him sitting at a table beside the immaculately kept kidney-shaped pool. A warm glow suffused her chest and heat rushed to her cheeks.

Was she happy to see him?

She wasn't sure. In normal circumstances she would have been, should have been, of course, but these were not normal circumstances…far from them.

* * * *

Luca lifted his gaze as Daniella approached. Pushing his chair back, he stood, removed his Oakley shades, and squinted from the bright sunlight. He looked her up and down as she glided closer toward him. She was a vision of beauty. But however beautiful she was, he had to stick to his plan and not be lured from it. Her hips sashayed from side to side with each step and the soft breeze caused a few loose curls to blow wildly behind her ears.

"Did you eat well? The staff prepared everything you wanted?" he asked, genuinely concerned. After all, it was in his best interests to keep her happy. Her being happy brought him one step closer to his revenge.

"Yes, thank you. It was lovely."

"The clothes were a perfect fit." Luca's gaze skimmed over the material that hugged her petite frame.

She brushed aside his compliment. "You've purchased some beautiful clothes. You really shouldn't have spent that much. They weren't necessary, Luca. I can go home and get my own."

"Firstly, this is now your home and you are not going back to Rocinha. And secondly, you needed maternity clothes. I doubt you have many of those?" He smiled and opened his palms to her as if closing a deal. He was treating her as if she was a regular Monday to Friday working day deal. Simple as that.

She licked her lips before speaking. "I appreciate your help yesterday, I really do, but…" She fiddled with the cardigan edging. "I'm not so sure about our arrangement now."

Luca leaned over the table, finished the final touches to his email and then shut the laptop down.

"We agreed you would stay here. I will look after you both." He looked down at her, small beside him.

"No, we didn't agree. You agreed with yourself. Yesterday, I was tired, emotional—" Daniella said, but he interrupted.

"Look, you are staying until then. I need to be sure you're both okay, *sim*?"

"But—"

"There are no buts, Daniella. You are my family, and it's my duty to take care of you. I'm not going to let you leave again."

Daniella tilted her head to the side and he could feel her almost hanging on to his last word. *Again.* His subconscious stepped into play and quizzed him. Was he referring to the day she'd walked out on him over five years ago or had it simply been a slip of the tongue? He mentally punished his subconscious for probing too deep. *Be quiet!*

He needed her here, with him twenty-four hours a day if his plan was to work. Not have her wandering off. He needed to seduce her and get her into his bed. He now realized it was going to take time, not the overnight plan he'd initially anticipated. But he would have her. He would take her body for himself, and then he would throw her away. A small whisper of a voice reminded him of the unborn child and his heart sank with guilt. No, he had to stay focused, whatever the cost. Revenge, he reminded himself. It would be sweet at the end.

Daniella started to shake. Her whole body trembled, right down to her toes.

"No," she said, shifting on the spot.

"No?" He was surprised that she continued to argue with him.

"No. You don't own me, Luca. I have had my fair share of being a prisoner to a Venancio, and it will not happen again. The baby and I will be fine." Her fists curled into tight balls, and her voice was full of determination.

He took a few slow steps toward her. "What do you mean you will not be a prisoner again?" he asked.

She fidgeted in front of him and shook her head as if arguing with herself.

"Your brother was no saint," she said, looking up at him with sorrowful eyes.

"I know that, but he tried to be good man. He won you over in the end, after all."

Daniella let out a soft laugh. "A good man? Would a good man do this?" She pointed to the bruising on her face. "Would a good man do this?" She pulled the cardigan aside to reveal scarring across her collarbone and shoulder. "I can continue if you'd wish?"

Luca saw her catch her breath as if she was

stopping herself from saying more.

"What are you saying?" He rubbed his jaw, which was still aching from yesterday's date with her palm. He was becoming more and more baffled trying to make sense of her words.

"Nothing." Daniella turned on her heel and started to retreat to the mansion. "Forget about it. I shouldn't have..." Her voice trailed off and he was unable to catch her last words.

Luca contemplated chasing after her, but instead he slumped back down into the wicker chair and held his head. What had just happened? What was Daniella suggesting? He had assumed his plan of revenge would be simple—gain her trust, seduce her, have her in his bed, and then discard her as if she meant nothing. It was foolproof, or so he'd thought.

He sucked in a deep breath and decided it was obvious that Daniella must have been fabricating her victim story. He didn't know where the bruising had come from exactly, but he was certain his brother would not have done such a thing. His own flesh and blood couldn't possibly have caused so much hurt and disrespect to his wife. He may have been involved in a lot of bad things when it came to his gang life, but he wouldn't hurt his wife. This was all part of her ploy to make Luca feel sorry for her, the innocent pregnant widow who needed support. He had to hand it to her, though, she was a fine actress and worthy of an Academy Award.

He sat up straight, replaced his designer shades, and smiled to himself. If she wanted to play dirty, he was ready. Hardball was his strong point. It would make the revenge all that much sweeter, and he couldn't wait to taste it.

Chapter 5

Luca insisted on taking her for the follow-up appointment with Dr. Menezes three days later, and now, Daniella stood clutching the black-and-white scan photograph. She'd wanted to protest about him taking her, but secretly a small part of her desperately wanted to see her baby again.

After it was finished, she was handed a small but perfect image of her growing child. The black-and-white 4D photograph clearly revealed her baby holding up four fingers and a thumb in front of his or her face. The small, but obviously Venancio trait nose was visible, but the little hand covered the rest of the face as if not wanting to be disturbed. A wave of emotion washed over Daniella as realization hit her hard.

The miracle of life was happening inside of her, and even if it had not been planned, she now realized her baby meant everything and more to her. Maternal instinct kicked in and the cruel conception suddenly seemed insignificant now that she had a life to care for.

This was her baby.

She held tightly on to the photograph with one hand

and rested the other on her tummy. She wouldn't let anyone, including Luca, take the child away from her. If that were what he had his mind set on, then she would be ready. She had protected herself from one brother and she could do it again.

Since arriving at Luca's home, she had made herself familiar with her new surroundings and its staff. Maria had been kind to her and was excited about the prospect of a new baby in the house. Daniella tried to explain that she and her baby wouldn't be staying long, but Maria laughed and told her that would change. "*Senhor* Venancio adores you, my dear."

She and Luca had exchanged few words since her revelation about Miguel's behavior.

Perhaps he didn't believe her?

She knew she'd once been the love of his life, but things had now changed.

Daniella turned her head and her heart raced uncontrollably like a butterfly trapped in her chest. His jaw was set tightly and his dark, brooding eyes were transfixed on the road as he concentrated on driving. His mocha-colored skin was clean-shaven and the smell of his masculine cologne filled her nostrils. Tearing her gaze away from him, she tried to compose herself, but his voice interrupted her.

"We are leaving for New York in the morning."

"We?"

"Yes, we."

"But… What…" New York. Her birthplace and home until the age of five. She could barely remember much of it, having been so young when she left. After her parents had passed away in a car accident, Daniella had been sent to stay with her paternal grandparents in Rio de Janeiro.

"I have an urgent meeting and I need to be in New York for it. In person," Luca explained as he turned the car into the driveway.

"Okay…but surely I can stay here? I don't need a bodyguard. Besides, you don't want me hassling you."

She looked from her shaking hand which still held the photo and back up at Luca. She wasn't sure how she felt about going back to New York, but her stomach was churning and she could feel the apprehension creeping upon her. She had lived with her grandparents in their town house and had never traveled outside of Rio. There had never been the opportunity. Until now.

"You will not be hassling me. Besides, I would like you to be nearby, so I can make sure that you are both okay. I checked with the doctor and she said it's fine for you to travel on this occasion. Humor me for a few more days?" Luca's gaze dropped to the photograph still held tightly in her hand.

"We will be fine, honest. Me…going along with you…it really isn't necessary."

She wasn't sure if she was ready to revisit the memories of losing her parents. She had only a couple of vivid memories of them and they were sweet. She didn't want to ruin them.

"Daniella, I know you're worried about traveling to New York, and believe me, if I could hold this meeting anywhere in the world, I would. Unfortunately, it is completely out of my hands and I have to be there. I can't, and I won't, leave you here alone. You're still getting your strength up and you need somebody around. After this trip, I will ensure all of my business is held in Rio."

"You mean I need you around?"

"*Exatamente*!"

* * * *

They had flown into the Newark airport on Luca's private jet last night and arrived at his apartment just after eight-thirty in the evening. His housekeeper had already prepared them a fine dinner of fillet steak, which he watched Daniella devour as her appetite returned. It was a severely cooler climate than Rio's and Luca had phoned ahead, out of earshot, and instructed his housekeeper to shop for some warmer clothing for Daniella's stay. He knew she would only object if she heard him make the call.

The next morning, he went straight to his office to meet with his associates. He had left Daniella asleep in the guest room and instructed his housekeeper, Rose, to keep an eye on her. He knew she was physically still not one hundred percent and bringing her back to New York could possibly weaken her emotionally. It was a gamble he had taken, but there was no other choice. He wasn't leaving her in Rio, miles away. She needed to be close wherever possible to strengthen his plan.

Luca focused on the meeting agenda and tried to put the sleeping beauty out of his mind. He engaged in the usual humdrum business conversations before sealing the deal. It had been taking shape over the last several weeks and now it was finalized. He had his hands on a generously large amount of Saudi's oil export and, after signing several pieces of watermarked paper, he pushed them back toward his attorney to settle up.

"Gentlemen, it was a pleasure doing business with you." He shook the hands of each of the men and turned to leave his office.

Collecting his cellphone and briefcase, Luca made his way out into the bitter winter air and straight into the warmth of his awaiting, chauffeur-driven Bentley. They traveled across the city, in the direction of his home on the outskirts of Midtown Manhattan. The sun's rays dazzled behind the skyscrapers and could have fooled anyone that it was the height of summer and not the midst of a record cold winter. The chauffeur parked the Bentley in the private basement and Luca took the elevator to his penthouse. He walked into the hallway and called out for Daniella. The apartment was silent and his voice echoed off of the chic whitewashed walls.

She has gone. Deus maldito! She was physically and emotionally weak and now she was AWOL in Manhattan. She was vulnerable in a city she didn't remember or know. Guilt started to consume him. How could he have let this happen?

Throwing the keys on to the Italian marble work surface, he strode into the lounge and found the fresh flowers he'd sent her earlier in the day placed in a crystal cut vase, which was perfectly positioned in the center of the coffee table beside the sofa.

There she was. Daniella was curled up on the sofa with her knees pulled up toward her chest. She had cocooned herself in one of the luxuriously soft bathrobes and a pair of his thick winter socks. Some of her curls had come loose from the band and framed her face, and her lashes fanned out in half circles and rested against the tops of her cheeks. Luca's heart thumped hard. She was safe. The accompanying note that had been delivered with the bouquet was held between her fingers.

Sleeping beauty, I didn't want to wake you. I will be back by lunchtime. L.

He crouched down beside her and settled his gaze on her lips, which were just parted as she softly breathed in and out. He inhaled deeply and reminded himself he needed to keep emotion out of this arrangement. Yes, she had the beauty of a goddess, but she also had the ability to change into a malicious enchantress.

Remember.

"Luca?" She began to stir and he came back to the present.

"*Sim.* I'm here, Daniella."

Her eyes were closed and she mumbled in her sleep, "No, Miguel, you can't hurt Luca. Please, I'll do anything."

He rested back on his haunches and realized she was talking in her sleep.

"Miguel, I beg you," she pleaded with his brother in her nightmares.

He considered whether to wake her as she was obviously dreaming.

Her eyebrows drew together, and frown lines formed across her forehead. A pained look crossed her face and her breathing quickened. She flung her arms across her face, as if protecting herself from something.

Or someone?

"No," she screamed.

Luca's gut wrenched and he wondered whether her story had been true and not just fabricated for his benefit.

"Daniella?" he whispered, stroking a finger down her cheek and meeting with a fresh teardrop.

She stirred under his touch and the frown lines faded gradually as she woke. "Luca?"

"I'm here." His words were soothing as he caressed her hair.

Her eyelids fluttered open and she looked up at him, confusion in her expression.

"I only sat down for a few minutes. I was going to give Rose a hand with lunch, but I must have fallen asleep."

"Don't worry. I'm sure she has it all under control. I'm glad you rested." Luca smiled.

She positioned a hand on her bump and looked up at him. "How was your morning?"

He sat back on the Italian leather sofa beside her and tried to process his racing thoughts. Her voice was loud, yet it was distant.

"Luca, what's wrong?"

"Huh?"

"I asked how your morning was?" she repeated her question, a look of curiosity on her face.

Images of her having the nightmare filled his mind, the genuine terror on her face now imprinted on his memory.

"Fantastic. I sealed the Saudi deal. Six months of tough negotiating and I finally got the figure I wanted. Plus a lot more." He placed his hand on top of hers. "So, we have great reason to celebrate. In fact, we are going out to celebrate properly. Tonight."

"Tonight? But—"

"Yes. I'm taking you to the best restaurant in New

York and we are celebrating the deal." Luca searched deep into her eyes. "And us." Now was the time to go back to his initial plan if he was going to achieve his goal.

"Us?" Her eyes opened wide.

"Yes, us. This is our second chance, Daniella. Don't you see that?" This was his chance to dangle the illusion of them reuniting as a couple, plant the seed and allow her to nurture it before he snatched it away.

She bit her bottom lip and worried it with her teeth. "And what about my baby?"

He took a deep breath and looked down at her hand, which was resting on top of the fluffy robe. Already she appeared fiercely protective of her child.

"I want you and the baby, *querida*." He surprised himself with the sincerity of his words, although he knew they were hollow lies. "You are one." Luca wanted to place his hand beside hers and feel the small curve of her belly and the life beneath it, but he stopped himself. He couldn't become too attached to either of them.

"You really mean that?"

"Yes. It was me who insisted you stay and I meant it, every word. All that has changed is I now want you both to stay and not leave after the baby is born," he explained. “Think about it.” His thumb grazed her bottom lip. “Think how we can be. This is our second chance.”

She was quiet for a moment before she answered. “I don’t know if us being together is the right thing—”

“I don’t care if it the right thing. If I had done the right thing five years ago, we wouldn’t be here now. I want you. All of you.” Luca grabbed her hips and lifted her in one swift movement so that she was straddling his lap.

She gasped and her body tensed, but she didn’t resist him.

“I don’t care about right and wrong. All I know is that I want you and anything and everything that comes with you.” He cupped her face with his hands and worked his fingers through her hair.

He clenched his jaw and resisted the desperate urge to take her there on the sofa, to use her body to satisfy his own needs. He wanted to tear the bathrobe off of her and taste her, inch by inch, taking what was rightfully his and should have been his years ago. Now, whatever he desired, he got immediately. He wasn’t used to having to wait patiently. The groundwork had to be done before he could claim the prize.

The time would come.

* * * *

Luca's throbbing pressed between her legs, his muscular thighs spreading her own apart. She focused on his dark eyes, the swirls of mahogany glistened in the light and she could see her dazed reflection in them. She wasn't ready for their relationship to progress and to open up to uncharted territory, rekindling both new and old feelings. Her confidence had been damaged and she wasn't sure if she could give everything to Luca wholeheartedly without believing in herself first.

She ran her tongue across her lips that had dried in the cool air of the lounge. New York was cold compared to her usual tropical climes. She had tried to figure out the heating system earlier but had given up after pushing at several buttons on the hi-tech control panel and having no luck.

"Luca. I…I don't know… I think…" She stumbled for words and shook her head.

He pulled her face down to meet his and whispered huskily, "Don't think." And pressed his lips against hers.

His long fingers pushed further into her hair, twisting through the curls and pulling her farther into the kiss. Letting out a soft moan, she found herself responding. Even though she wanted to stop and pull away, a small part of her felt at home at last. She was kissing the man she loved. She wasn't scared by his touch and didn't need to withdraw and protect herself. Her body melted into his embrace.

One hand rested on his chest and the other wrapped around his neck. She wanted to place her hands on his bare skin and feel the rise and fall of his breath. It was something so simple, yet essential to survive. She needed to feel the life in him. Daniella choked back the fear that had consumed her for five years. The fear that she would never see him again. Alive. To watch him breathe right in front of her was a beauty in itself.

His hands moved from her hair and traced down her cheeks, her neck, and rested on her shoulders. Her skin heated and the desire for his caresses built within her. He tucked his thumbs under the edge of the collar of her bathrobe and gently pushed it away, revealing just a thin camisole top and lacy briefs. He let out a muffled groan and when he ran his hands along the length of her shoulders and arms, the tiny hairs across her body stood tall and gooseflesh covered her skin.

Her heart was racing, and her breaths were quick and shallow. She had to stop this from going any further.

As much as she wanted to, she knew she wasn't ready. She wasn't sure she would ever be.

"Luca…I think…we…" She tried to say the words, but putting words together had become very hard.

He pulled her closer to him, his strong hands on her hips as he pushed the robe aside.

She let her head fall back slightly and murmured against him. "Luca, please."

Was she begging him to stop or continue? Her head spun faster but she was well aware of where his hands were traveling as they glided lower.

Stop. Just say it.

Her inner voice chastised her. Why couldn't she say the simple four-lettered word, stop.

She didn't want to upset Luca. Over the years, silent cooperation had become an automatic response, yet she desperately tried to find the strength and voice within her.

"Luca…"

She still couldn't bring herself to say it. Her body was electrified with tingling pleasure. Her nipples betrayed her and hardened against his soft, yet wickedly rough hands as he gently cupped her breasts. His touch was welcomed, and she arched her back and pushed herself into his hold. She needed to bring this to a halt before it went any further, but it was so exquisite and natural. His touch didn't frighten her, it didn't hurt her, and it didn't mark her. It was how a lover's embrace should be. A liquid sensation curled in the depths of her belly, and she knew she had to stop him right now. Although she trusted Luca, she needed time to regain her confidence and heal from what his brother had subjected her to. Throwing herself into another relationship wasn't the answer, even if it was with the love of her life.

Oh, dear God. Just say it.

Mustering all the strength she had left, she whispered, "Stop."

His hands immediately stilled, and he looked at her, not saying a word.

Please don't be angry.

His gaze rested on hers and he shuffled in his seat a little. He didn't look angry. Of course he wouldn't be. The Luca she knew had morals and understanding. He cared—not like his twisted sibling.

"I just…I just think we…"

"We what?" he asked gently.

"I can't do this…not yet."

His eyebrows pulled closely together in a frown and

then quickly eased apart. He wasn't angry, maybe frustrated, but not angry she concluded. He was a gentleman.

"I just want to take it slowly, please. My head is full of…" She brought her hands to her head and rubbed her temples. "Well, let's just say it's a mixed up place at the moment." An uneasy silence lingered between them both for several minutes before Daniella spoke again. "But being with you is helping it all to make sense a little more. Please, be patient with me."

She wasn't sure if a flash of uncertainty crossed his face, but before she could blink, it was gone. Maybe she had imagined it.

"I am still taking you out tonight and treating you like a queen. What does your heart desire? You name it and you will find it here."

He checked his cellphone and then placed it back into his jacket pocket. She was sure he wasn't used to be rejected and his ego was probably now feeling a little bruised.

"Umm, I don't mind. You choose."

"No, it's your choice."

"Okay." She paused for a moment. "Well, I would really like to eat some *feijoada*." She was craving the typical Brazilian stew and had been since stepping off the jet yesterday afternoon.

Luca's laugh echoed throughout the room. "You have flown hundreds of miles and you want to eat *feijoada*, seriously?"

"Yes. It's what the baby wants," she protested. It was one of her favorite meals and full of goodness, though she highly doubted they would find it in New York.

Luca nodded. "*Certamente!* Whatever the baby would like, she will have. I know just the place."

* * * *

"Thank you, sir, most kind of you," gushed the headwaiter as Luca paid for the meal and handed the waiter a more than generous tip.

Daniella shrugged into the thick, black designer coat Luca was holding out for her and shivered as his fingers brushed against her.

"Are you okay?" Luca asked.

"Yes. Yes, I'm fine," she answered, conscious of people looking at her as they had been all evening. "Why is everyone staring at me?" she whispered and leaned in closer to him.

He placed his hand around her waist and lowered

his head to reach her level. "Because you are the most beautiful woman in this room."

The warmth of his breath made her shudder and gasp to catch her own. She was sure everyone was looking at them because they were aware of who Luca was and because of his undeniable good looks. They probably wondered who the short, unpolished, pregnant woman on his arm was. She pushed the thought aside and found herself lost in his words, wanting to believe them. For once, she wanted to imagine a man could say and mean such tender words and not expect anything in return. After all, he had once loved her for everything she was.

"Ready?" He interrupted her daydream and extended his hand for hers.

She smiled and accepted his hand.

"*Adeus*, *Senhor* Venancio." The concierge held the door and nodded to them both.

"You come here often?"

"Occasionally."

By the way staff and visitors had reacted and treated them, she was sure it was fairly regularly. Perhaps he missed his motherland of Brazil more than he liked to admit and sought solace in this quirky yet familiar Brazilian restaurant.

The cold air hit Daniella's face with such sharpness that a small cry escaped her lips. She could feel her loose curls being blown in every direction. *Damn.*

"Come here." He shrugged out his coat and draped it over her shoulders.

He drew her close to his solid warmth and she was thankful for the protection his body offered. Icy air filled her nostrils and stung her throat as she breathed in.

"Thank you for the meal. It was delicious. I don't think I need to eat for a week now."

"You're welcome. Let's get you home and warmed up." He started to guide her in the direction of the chauffeur-driven Chrysler, which was pulling into one of the waiting bays.

Daniella took a step out into the empty road and felt herself being pulled away from Luca's warm embrace. As if in slow motion, her purse was snatched from her shoulder and she was pushed to the hard ground.

Chapter 6

"Hey!" Luca roared at the young kid running away with Daniella's purse.

Daniella. Was she hurt? Was the baby okay? He held her gently and looked into her face. She didn't appear to be in any pain.

"I'm okay. I'm fine," she reassured him, sensing his question. Her voice was shaky and her bright green eyes were wide with fear.

With his free hand he helped Daniella back on to her feet and supported her as she stood.

"Are you hurt? Are you sure you're okay?" He cupped her face in his hands.

"Yes, I'm fine."

"Go to the car, now." He let go of her and started to move away.

"Luca, please no. Leave it—"

Luca sprinted down the walkway and turned the corner, following the boy's tracks. He was physically fit and the adrenaline spurred him on even further. The kid was in his sight. Luca's arms moved at his sides, pushing him faster toward his target.

He reached out and grabbed the boy's coat collar and instantly brought him to a halt. His heart pounded and he was poised to fight, to protect, the adrenaline filled his veins within seconds.

He faced the troublesome kid, pushing him against the wall. He was young; he looked about fourteen or fifteen, and Luca found himself remembering his early teenage years and his own relationship with trouble and felony. He battled internally. Did he want to help this boy who could have potentially harmed Daniella and the baby, or did he want to hand him over?

"Luca…" Daniella's voice called from several meters away.

"I said to wait in the car. Go back, Daniella."

"No." Her voice wavered.

Luca sucked in a deep breath and fought back the urge to argue with her there and then.

"You owe this lady an apology," he said calmly to the boy, giving himself a few more seconds to think.

The boy lifted his head and met Daniella's gaze. A remorseful expression was evident on his face.

"Sorry, miss." He extended the purse to her. "I didn't mean to hurt you. I just needed some food."

Luca dropped his hands from the boy's shoulders

and hesitated for several seconds before reaching into his jacket pocket and retrieving a business card.

"If you really want to sort yourself out, call here tomorrow morning. Otherwise, I will press charges." He removed the boy's cellphone from his hand and waved it in front of him. "Insurance policy."

The boy took the card offered and scampered away, looking back over his shoulder.

"What are you doing? Are you going to let him get away?" Daniella cried.

"Come on, let's just get home," Luca said, taking her hand and pulling her gently toward the car.

"No," she protested, and snatched her hand away from his grip.

"Daniella, come on. He was just a kid and…"

"A kid who should know better! You call that…this…looking after my child and me? He tried to openly mug me on the street and then you rewarded him for it!" She stared at him and held his gaze.

He waited a moment and thought before he spoke.

She was right. Yes, it was an unorthodox way of handling such a situation, but he was prepared to take the chance, and if it failed he had the boy's personal details and would follow through with pressing charges.

"Let me handle this my way, Daniella." His voice was firm.

"Some people are simply beyond any help at all." She turned her back on him and walked to the car. He wondered whom her bitter comment was really meant for.

* * * *

The elevator to his penthouse home was ridden in silence. Luca turned the key, pushed the door open, and signaled for her to enter before him. He knew she thought badly of his earlier actions, and he was well aware that he was going to have to work hard to repair the damage.

One step forward and two steps back.

"I'm going to bed." She walked down the hallway toward the room he'd shown her earlier. "Good night." Her icy tone sent a shiver down his spine.

He shoved his hands in his trouser pockets and clenched his jaw. It still ached slightly. Though he had deserved it and more. The soft click of the guest bedroom door jolted him back to the present.

He couldn't allow arguments to keep interrupting his plan for revenge. Then he smiled as he had a sudden thought. He could use Daniella's unhappiness to his advantage. He must swallow his pride and let her think she was in control. He had to get her back on his side. He had thought his plan would be swift and painless, but to his surprise it was requiring a great deal of his time. All he had to do was make her fall back in love with him, share his bed for the night, and then leave her. It was foolproof. She was a widow, fragile and emotional. It was his opportunity to be acting as the support she needed. He would apologize through gritted teeth and be the rock she obviously needed. She must trust him wholeheartedly before he could discard her like trash. He released the knot of his tie and threw the silk fabric on to the sofa. Just like she had done to him.

He poured himself a single measure of fine whiskey into a crystal tumbler and brought it to his lips. The heat numbed his throat as he savored the expensive taste. The spectacular panoramic view of New York beckoned him. He opened the sliding glass door and stepped out onto the balcony. The sounds of steadily flowing traffic filled the cold air that whipped at his cheeks. He took another sip of the liquor and was thankful for the warmth it gave to his throat and stomach. New York had welcomed him wholeheartedly just over five years ago when he had made the choice to leave Brazil. Now it was his home and Brazil…was a lifetime ago.

It was ironic he had chosen to set up home in the very state Daniella had been born in. Perhaps he had been influenced subconsciously?

He would stay in Rio for the exact amount of time it took to have his revenge and then he would be on the first flight out. There was nothing to bind him to that part of the world any longer.

The skyline dazzled with thousands of lights, shining from various offices, homes, and street lamps. They illuminated the onyx black sky and reflected in the Hudson River far below him. Why would he want to go back to Rio to stay when he had all of this? He tried to convince himself as he threw back the last of the liquor.

Luca closed the balcony door and strolled toward Daniella's room. The sound of the shower running signaled she wasn't asleep and his mind filled with images of her naked body covered in droplets of water, her hair slick down the curve of her back. *Focus!*

He opened the door quietly and entered her room. The en-suite door was ajar and steam swirled through the small gap. Luca followed the floral scent, which filled the humid air around him. He knew he was invading her privacy when he pushed gently against the open door, but he couldn't help it. His primitive instincts were leading him astray. Steam poured out of the room and surrounded him, dampening his shirt. He took a couple steps into the bathroom and tried to make out Daniella's silhouette through the mist. Her voice broke the silence as she started to hum a tune. He leaned casually against the basin and crossed his ankles. With the en-suite door now open the steam was thinning and the shower door panel was becoming transparent

Her back was turned, and her curls had disappeared; her hair was smooth and slick over her shoulders and down the length of her back. A primeval need overcame him—he wanted to take her in the shower, against the glass windowpane, fast and slow.

No.

He needed patience and plenty of it.

Not tonight. But surely he could indulge in a small appetizer?

Luca watched as she bent over slightly to turn off the faucet, unaware that she was teasing him with her curves. He picked up one of the soft Egyptian cotton towels stacked on the shelf and had it ready to hand to her. He was meant to be playing the part of a gentleman, after all.

* * * *

Daniella sighed as she ran her hands over her wet hair, wringing it out to the side. The water had relaxed her mind, body, and soul, and prepared her for sleep. Returning to New York had been an emotional move. Now back in the city that never sleeps, she was unsure of herself and didn't know how to manage her feelings. She felt guilty for not being able to remember her parents and happy family memories. Part of her wished she'd stayed in Rio. It was all she had known for the last twenty years. She reached for the handle and slid the door aside.

The scream left her lips as soon as she laid eyes on the man in front of her. Luca was mere inches from her, casually resting against the basin as if he had the God-given right to be there.

"What are you doing? Get out!" She attempted to cover her body with her hands.

His gaze wandered across her body, burning into her skin. She stood naked in front of him and was completely exposed to his gaze

His lips curved upward, a playful smirk settling upon them. He hesitated for a moment before extending the towel to her. "Here."

"Get out!" she repeated, snatching the towel away from him and holding it tightly against her body.

He stepped forward and stood close to her. She kept her gaze on him. His stare was so intense that she was beginning to feel faint. Out of the corner of her eye she saw him remove his hands from his trouser pockets and reach up for her towel…her shield from him.

He gently tugged on the material and before she realized it had slipped from her hands and he had tossed it across the bathroom.

"I'm not ready to leave yet." His words were said with such intensity, she knew he was serious. She caught sight of her reflection in the mirror, and fear and anger filled her face.

He placed both his hands on the side of the shower doorframe and leaned toward her, blocking her only exit. She let her gaze fall on his parted lips; their softness called to her. He stepped up into the shower, his clothed body now touching her slick, wet skin. Daniella moved back but her shoulders and buttocks met the cold, tiled wall. She had no way of escaping, even if she'd wanted to. A small part of herself wanted him closer, needed him against her, his strong hands on her body once more.

Luca took hold of her wrists and held them gently,

but firmly, just above her head. "You are…so beautiful…Daniella," he whispered as he placed soft kisses along her jaw before his open mouth met her lips.

She could feel herself giving into his touch. Her mind raced, battling to remain strong and not cave in as she responded to his hot lips. He held her hands higher against the tiles, and her shoulders and breasts rose and fell with the each breath she fought to suck in. He broke away from the kiss and lowered his head to meet her right breast. Taking her erect and sensitive nipple between his lips, Luca grazed his tongue over the small bud and teased it gently between his teeth, adding just enough pressure to make her to cry out with pleasure. Daniella wanted to be released so she could be free to run her hands over his muscular chest and dig her nails into his golden flesh as he brought her closer to the edge.

As if he knew her thoughts, Luca let go of one hand and traced his own down the outline of her body, skimming over her full breasts and hips. He nudged her softly and she felt his hand between her thighs. Her body stiffened automatically and she closed her eyes.

He won't hurt me, he won't hurt me.

The niggling thought at the back of her mind was there to remind her of Miguel and his violent attacks upon her. She wanted to tell Luca, but couldn't even say it out loud to herself. She had told nobody, as instructed by her late husband. He had repeatedly taken her against her will. He had raped her, his wife, yet she still had to maintain the perfect marriage façade even though he was now dead.

"Relax," Luca whispered into her ear, the stubble on his jaw scratching her cheek.

She tried to relax, but her body was not cooperating with her brain. The last five years she had been told not to argue back, not to think, to not have a say in any matter. Now having freedom, she was completely ill-equipped to use it.

His hand settled on her hip and interrupted her thoughts. He released her second hand and cupped her face with both.

"I'm sorry. Forgive me, *querida*. I shouldn't have done this." He rested his forehead against hers. "It seems I cannot control myself around you."

Daniella draped her arms around his neck and held him tightly against her body. Words escaped her. How could she tell him that she desperately wanted him, physically needed him, but mentally she wasn't ready? She couldn't find a way to explain that his brother had left her unable to trust, that she was full of fear to even be near another man. *I just can't tell him.*

Firstly, she couldn't find the words or the courage. Second, what was the point when Luca would just accuse her of making up vicious lies about his brother? Even though they had a volatile relationship, he still wouldn't believe what she had to say about Miguel. Or perhaps, more to the point, he did not want to believe her. In his eyes, she had left him, rejected him for his sibling.

"It won't happen again." He took her hands and kissed them. "I'll leave you to get some sleep."

* * * *

Early the next morning, Daniella sat at the kitchen breakfast bar and looked down at the steaming mug of coffee that Rose handed to her. Daniella stirred in some extra milk.

"Coffee always starts my morning off beautifully." Luca took a mouthful of his own just-black coffee.

He wore another sharp gray suit, with a royal navy shirt and tie. It fit his body perfectly and made him look as if he had stepped right out of the latest copy of *GQ*.

"Mmm," she agreed, and nodded toward the housekeeper who was busying herself with breakfast.

"Thank you, Rose."

The hot liquid traveled down her throat and hit her empty stomach, filling it with luxurious warmth. Her tummy made a loud rumble as she watched Rose cooking bacon and eggs. She returned her gaze to Luca and asked, "So, what is the plan today?"

"I have to go back into work for a few hours, and you will be coming with me."

"Oh, Luca, please, not this again. You don't need to watch my every single move. I'm fine staying right here."

"It will do you some good to get out and have a change of scenery for more than an evening. Some daylight, some sunshine. Fresh air in your lungs."

He did have a point. She had only stepped out of the building for a couple of hours last night. She looked over her shoulder toward the enormous lounge windows. The sun was rising over the skyscrapers that made up the city.

Why was she reluctant? Last night's actions had shaken her, yes, but it was more than that. She was scared to embrace New York. Frightened that she would remember it and her parents and then be left with nothing concrete to hold on to. To remember was dangerous. To let herself feel was just insanity. She had been through enough heartache to last her a lifetime and wasn't sure if she had any room for more. Staying put at Luca's home, surrounded by the safety of walls until it was time to leave for Rio, suited her fine.

"I don't want to go out. I'm happy to stay here and…help Rose."

Luca tilted his head to the side and watched her intently. Was she some sort of behavior study to him? She couldn't figure him out.

"I think she has it covered here. It's just for a couple of hours, then we can do whatever you would like this afternoon, *sim*?"

He kept his gaze on her eyes and didn't blink. Was this his tactic to see who would look away first or was he trying to genuinely understand her? His gaze was fixed on hers and neither blinked. His stare didn't falter and remained intense, she felt it almost searing through to her soul and her heart responded. But she was still uneasy and the heat spread to her cheeks. She hated being the center of attention and right now his total attention was on her.

"Okay." She was the first to look away. "I'll go if it means that much to you."

They finished their breakfast and Daniella retreated to her room to wash and dress whilst Luca glanced through a new work proposal. She opened the wardrobe and saw outfit after outfit with suitable adjustments for the third trimester of her pregnancy. Even though having Luca flashing his cash about frustrated and annoyed her, she admitted it was a nice gesture and extremely thoughtful. She dressed quickly, slipping on black, chunky knit tights and a plum-colored, cashmere, knee-length dress. She looked in the mirror and admired her now obviously accentuated bump.

Luca guided her to the elevator and down to the basement garage. He placed his warm hand on the small of her back as they walked side by side. Daniella shuddered as goose bumps covered her body, independently reacting to his touch.

Luca greeted his on-hand chauffeur in the building's reserved car park. "I won't be needing you today."

Once Daniella had fastened her seatbelt, he fired up the engine and smiled at her. "Beautiful, isn't she? Let me introduce my baby, my Bugatti Veyron 16.4."

Daniella watched his playful smile and teased him. "Boys and their toys. Is this supposed to impress me?"

She was enjoying the flirtatious banter between them and shrugged off the embarrassment of yesterday's moments in the shower.

He laughed. "No, but I know it does."

Luca drove through the city streets with confidence, quickly weaving the impressive vehicle in and out of the lanes. She watched him change the gears; he certainly knew how to handle the fast car. She felt safe and smiled grimly as she thought he had complete control over the vehicle, just like he did over her. Closing her eyes, she remembered his hands on her yesterday and the passion he had held back. She opened her eyes and forced herself to look out of the window.

Focus on something else and not him!

* * * *

Luca led her to a row of glass elevators. They crossed the marble floor of the reception foyer, passing by the group of immaculately groomed administration staff. Luca saw a couple of them glance toward Daniella and his hand on the small of her back as he guided her. Once they were out of view inside the elevator, she pulled her coat tightly around her. "I feel like a goldfish in here. When you designed this place, why did you choose glass for everything? Even at your home here and in Rio, why is that?"

Luca put his hands in his pockets and took a couple of steps around the capsule shape. "Truthfully?"

She shrugged. "Of course."

"Well, to be honest, it reminded me of you. You loved the light and open spaces and I just took that with me."

He realized it was ludicrous to have held onto her, even though he couldn't have her, but he had kept a small part of her with him wherever he went. He'd just had to. He simply couldn't let go of her and forget. He needed to get her out of his system once and for all.

Remember why you're doing this.

Fabricated images of Daniella and Miguel played in slow motion in his mind as his gut tightly knotted. He couldn't bear to consider the two of them together, the two of them being intimate. She had been his and then simply dumped him like trash for his brother. He needed to focus and not fall for her pity-me illusion.

She stared at him for a moment before reaching for his hand. "Oh, Luca. I don't know what to say. I…I'm sorry. I had to—"

"Shh." He placed his finger against her lips to silence her. "It doesn't matter. Anyway, I kind of like the light myself. Vitamin D, right?"

Daniella frowned and kept hold of his hand. She stared silently through the glass as they rode toward the top floors. The doors glided open and his personal secretary, Jude, greeted them from behind her desk. She was leggy and slim, a catwalk model like with honey blonde hair down to her waist. The perfect rouge lipstick had been applied to her pouty lips and matched her long, well-manicured fingernails. She fit in amongst his work life and environment perfectly. Immaculate. Controlled. Flawless. Luca knew that she desired him, but it would never be in the cards. She was good at her job, and exceedingly nice on the eye, but that was where it ended. Work and private life were kept completely separate on all accounts.

"Good morning, sir…madam?" She nodded at Daniella with raised eyebrows. Luca had never brought guests into his office before, not even his associates. The meetings were always held in the boardroom. His office was his space alone, yet there he was bringing his ex-lover into it. He could see the look of surprise on Jude's face.

* * * *

Three hours later, Luca glanced across to where

Daniella was sitting cross-legged on the armchair. She had shuffled it around, positioning it so it faced out of the window to look upon the city below. She'd silently sat in that same position since he had started to work.

"I'm all done here. Why don't we go and get some lunch?"

She broke her intense gaze with the city's horizon and looked him directly in the eye. "Can I ask you something?"

"Anything. Fire away." He crouched beside the chair and waited for her to speak. Her eyes were open wide and appeared a deeper shade of green than usual. They were entrancing and captured him.

"Why did you let that boy just walk away last night?"

Luca ran his hand through his hair and down over his face as he sighed. "I didn't just let him walk away. Do you think that was an easy decision? You…you and the child are my first and foremost priority. Believe me."

Her gaze was firmly fixed on his now and her eyebrows rose in question. He owed her a clearer explanation.

"Daniella, when we were together before, there were things I never told you."

"Yes, I know."

"Although Miguel so kindly filled in a lot of the spaces on my behalf..." He took hold of her hand. "Did he tell you about how I found my way into business exactly?"

She fidgeted in the seat. "No, he didn't give me details, but he said something about you being given everything and not earning it."

"*Sim*. I guess he would say that." Anger rose in his gut and he tried to tone down the level of sarcasm his tone held. He paused for a moment and concentrated on her hand in his. "That's not true. I have worked my ass off for every single cent I have. I was not given anything on a silver platter as Miguel cared to make out. What I was offered was a chance…an opportunity to better myself."

"You always told me that you had won some sort of scholarship?"

"I know, and I am sorry that I wasn't entirely honest with you back then. Perhaps I was ashamed of the actual facts." He took a deep breath. "I was exactly the same as that kid the other night, Daniella. I pickpocketed, I thieved, hell I did all sorts that I'm not proud of. Things I didn't want you to know about.

Maybe lucky for me, but the last guy I stole from was a successful businessman who saw perhaps the smallest glimmer of hope for me. He offered me a chance to repay for my behavior and earn a living away from the streets."

Her eyebrows drew together as she stared back at him and her hand twitched under his own. The man's words still rang clearly in his mind from all those years ago. *We all deserve a second chance. Take it kid, because there definitely won't be a third.*

"I see," Daniella whispered.

"That boy…well, I just wanted to believe that some good could come out of a bad situation. It worked for me. I saw a little of myself in him and wanted to do the best I could. You and the baby were okay. Believe me, if you had been hurt in the slightest, I would have dealt with him once and for all. You have to trust me."

His heart pounded and the unfamiliar feeling of opening up to others filled him with unease. Although Daniella and he had shared a life together before, he had never disclosed much about his youth to her, or anyone. He was still ashamed of the kid…the man he had been, but right now those memories were needed and they could help him with another step toward his plan.

"Okay." She smiled timidly at him and tucked a loose curl behind her ear. "I can't say I agree with what you did, but I can now understand the reasoning as to why a little more. Thank you for being honest with me."

Luca's heart softened in response to her innocent expression. He closed his eyes to sever their link. The warmth in his heart was quickly replaced by the all too familiar cold and icy grip.

Just like when he left her room last night. Luca had rested the back of his head against her door. He had gotten her back on his side, he was sure of it. Although frustrated, he'd smiled and gone back to his room at that point.

Admittedly, he'd thought she would be an easier conquest than this, but what was the saying? Good things come to those who wait?

Chapter 7

"Is this really necessary?" Daniella touched the soft, silky fabric covering her eyes.

"Completely. It's a surprise." Luca's tone was playful, relaxed, far from the usual serious and matter-of-fact composure she was used to hearing.

"So, you're happy with the nursery? Everything is as you want it?" He leaned over her, buckled her seat belt, and then his own.

Three weeks had passed since they'd left New York and returned to Rio. Luca had organized his schedule to work from home and insisted she choose a room and decorate it as a nursery. Luca had hired a small team of professional designers and decorators to assist under her direction, which had resulted in a beautiful and serene space just opposite her bedroom.

"It's beautiful…no, it's stunning. I couldn't imagine it being any more perfect than it already is."

Before leaving the house that morning, she'd run her fingertips along the soft, freshly polished oak cot and smiled. It was a nursery fit for a princess…or prince, she corrected herself. She was still unaware of the sex of her baby. She'd deliberately chosen neutral colors instead of pink or blue. Deep shades of chocolate-browns, off-whites, and creams were teamed with solid oak furniture to complete the homecoming suite for her little one.

"You haven't touched the account I've set up for you."

"I've told you it was unnecessary. I have a little money. Plus, so far you haven't given me a chance to pay for anything!"

"Well, as long as you know that the money is yours for whenever you need it."

Daniella nodded her head in reply.

"Good. As long as you're happy, I'm happy."

Today, he had insisted on no work and just play.

"Can't you just tell me where we're going now? This is silly. I look ridiculous."

"Why are you worried? Nobody can see you." He tapped lightly against the blacked-out windows of the Bentley and reminded her of the privacy it offered.

"Well, you can see me." She attempted to blindly point in his direction.

He shuffled beside her and, without being able to see, she still knew his gaze was on her, scorching her skin. Heat rose to her cheeks and she became even more aware of the material covering her eyes. The silky fabric brushed delicately against her lashes and tops of her eyelids. Her pulse raced at the uncertainty of their location.

"And what is wrong with me seeing you?"

His voice, as soft as the silk, whispered quietly and her heart fluttered. How could his raspy, accentuated voice and a piece of silk affect her so deeply? So physically. She twisted her hands in her lap and tried to focus on something else.

"It's not fair that I can't see you. I feel…I…" She stumbled for the words. "I feel exposed like this. You're looking at me and—"

"Who says I'm looking at you?" His voice was low and his warm breath on her skin sent shivers tingling down her spine.

Daniella swallowed and attempted to compose herself.

It was true. The blindfold left her vulnerable, yet strangely exhilarated. He was now so close to her face—her lips, his hot breath warming her skin.

Is he going to kiss me?

Her heart pounded so loud, she was sure even the chauffeur could hear it. An exquisite sensation pulled deep within her belly and she caught her breath. The telltale moisture at the very top of her thighs was instantly met with embarrassment as heat continued to rise to her cheeks—it happened every time she thought of Luca recently, and she couldn't keep blaming everything on her pregnancy hormones. She was positive he would have had the exact same effect whether she was nearly eight months pregnant or not.

This wanton need for him had taken over her body and soul and left her mind vacant. She couldn't find words, but Daniella knew she wanted him more than anything else in the world. Unclasping her hands, she slowly reached out beside of her. Her fingertips instantly came into contact with his face and confirmed her earlier thoughts of his closeness. Uncontrollable fluttering in her stomach took over as her fingers traced his skin, soft and smooth from the fresh shave earlier that morning. Her trembling hand cradled his cheek as she lingered in the moment.

"This is not the first time your hand has been in contact with my face, so why are you shaking, *querida*?"

Daniella giggled and was thankful for his lighthearted humor as she recalled the harsh slap across his cheek she had given him in the hospital suite. The blindfold was giving her courage and she longed for his lips on to be on hers. It was as necessary to her as the very air she breathed.

"What do you want, what does your heart desire, Daniella?" His lips grazed her earlobe as he leaned in closer, and she shuddered at the gentle touch.

She caught her bottom lip between her teeth and rolled it gently from side to side before she spoke. What did she want?

All of him. His lips on hers. His tongue exploring her mouth. His hands on her body. She wanted him in between of her legs and making her…

No. Not in the car, in public.

She reined in her wild imagination and fought for control.

"I want…I…need you to kiss me," she whispered. The blindfold offered her a sense of security, protection. If he objected, she wouldn't have to face the rejection in his eyes. *There, I've said it.* She breathed a sigh of relief.

One hand cupped her cheek and his thumb traced over her parted lips. His lips met with her cheek and trailed small caresses against her burning skin. "Relax," he murmured against her cheek.

Daniella arched her back and pressed herself into

his embrace as his lips finally met hers. With a small moan of pleasure, she draped both arms around Luca's neck. His mouth pushed onto hers with wild intensity and her lips tingled with the slightest hint of pleasurable pain. His free hand traced up and over her hips, her waist, and cupped her breast. Soft whispers, which she couldn't understand, warmed her lips. She was sure she heard him mutter something under his breath, but she couldn't make out what exactly. Her heart beat like a drum in her chest and filled her ears. As she relaxed, Luca's tongue invaded and explored her mouth, entwining with her own. He was in control now, directing the embrace, stamping his ownership on her mouth and physique. Adrenaline pumped through her body and her skin prickled with excitement.

She longed for his hands to explore her body, for his fingers to tease between her legs. She was ready for him now and needed to let him know.

Daniella pulled back and away from his mouth. "Luca, I—"

He leaned forward to cover her lips with his once again, pushing harder to prevent her from finishing her words.

He slowed and his hot lips leisurely pulled away

from her. "As much as I want to have you here, right now, more than anything…we can't. All in good time, I promise you."

With her vision clouded, it was hard to concentrate on his voice. She licked her tingling lips and nodded.

He rested his forehead against hers. "*Meu Deus!* Do you realize what you do to me, Daniella?"

He shuffled again, presumably rearranging himself, and she smiled to herself.

"Can I please take this silly thing off now?" She reached for the blindfold.

"Yes, you can. We're here."

"Where exactly?"

Luca released the tie at the back of her head and pocketed the silky fabric. "See for yourself."

Daniella turned to the window and fear crawled into her throat. Several ladies dressed in carnival attire sauntered past their vehicle and toward the crowd of people enjoying Rio carnival.

"You said we were going somewhere safe." Panic gripped her throat.

"How much safer do you want? This place is swarming with security." He tried to tease her.

"That's not what I meant." She grabbed his hand.

Luca's gaze fell on her grasp. "Then what do you mean? Tell me. I cannot keep attempting to translate your cryptic clues. Why is the carnival not safe? You can't stay cooped up at home all of the time." His gaze lingered on her tummy for a few seconds before he spoke. "It's not good for either of you."

She sucked in a quick breath and looked from him back to the crowds outside. Her mind raced as fear consumed her. Miguel had made it clear to Daniella that if Luca returned to Brazil he would end Luca's life. *But Miguel isn't here anymore.* Her inner voice attempted to reassure her, but she couldn't entirely block out the constant replay of her and Luca's parting.

Being forced to lie to Luca, she'd had to tell him that she no longer loved him. She'd had no choice but to go along with Miguel's wicked plans, as she knew his violent gang was more than capable of following through with his demands. Daniella knew this was the last time she would see Luca as he stood on the doorstep to his favela childhood home, his expressive eyes fixed on her.

"You are leaving me, for this?" He gestured to the men surrounding them. Weapons were loaded and

pointed at the ready under Miguel's orders.

"Leave me alone, Luca. I don't want to be with you...I don't love you anymore. Just leave me, leave here and don't come back." The premeditated words sickened her and she almost choked as she whispered them one by one, watching as pain and anguish filled his expression.

She turned to face the man who was blackmailing her into marriage and using her to torture his brother. The brother he hated and despised; the jealousy uncontrollable inside of him.

"I love Miguel." She pressed her mouth to his cold lips as he pulled her to him possessively.

She forced herself to hold back the flood of tears and loathing for the man who groped at her as if he now possessed her like a new pet. Miguel's cruel fingers held her close to him and Luca walked away from her, pain and hurt in every line of his body. He strode away and then slammed his fist in the hood of his car, making a huge dent.

"Tell me what's wrong." Luca's voice pulled her back to the present. "I thought you would like it...or is that another thing that has changed about you?"

Apart from the tiny furrow in his brow, his face was

relaxed and he appeared genuinely excited about their destination, throwing fleeting glances toward the celebrations. She took a calming breath and rested her palm on top of her small bump.

Who said that any of Miguel's gang would even be at the carnival? The *favela* was their stomping ground, and they would never venture out of it to a place like the carnival. She was overreacting and needed to forget the last five years.

Calm down and enjoy yourself. Luca won't let anything happen.

"Okay." She forced a smile to her face and attempted to invent an excuse for her overreaction. "I'm sorry. I didn't mean to be ungrateful or rude—"

"There's nothing to be sorry for." He squeezed her hand.

Her memories of Miguel faded and she concentrated all of her energy on the present.

Luca reached into his trouser pocket and retrieved his cellphone. As he stepped out of the car and made his way around to open her door, Daniella briefly heard him talk, but the exact conversation failed her earshot. He had pocketed the phone by the time he had reached her car door.

"Who was that?"

"Nothing for you to worry about. Now come on, we've already missed the beginning and the middle, not that it really matters because we both know the end is the best part."

Luca beamed like a joyful child as he kissed the back of her hand. It was one of the first times she'd seen him let down his guard; he was completely relaxed.

* * * *

Their earlier kiss reminded Luca of their time together years ago. He'd always loved Daniella and he knew deep inside he could never stop loving her. It was impossible. She was in his blood, imprinted on his soul, and carved on his heart.

No. Stop. He reined himself in. He wouldn't be distracted by one mere kiss.

She wanted something from him. Something physical. He smiled to himself; one point to him. She was exactly where he'd hoped for her to be at this stage of his plan, trusting and wanting him. He shook off the uncomfortable twinge bothering him.

"Let's have some fun today. No dramas, no business, just you and me. *Sim*?"

"*Sim*." She smiled at Luca and held on tightly to his

hand as he guided her toward one of the *camarotes* luxury suites of the Sambodromo stadium.

He nodded in the direction of the *camarotes*. "I thought it would be more ideal given you are nearly ready to give birth. It's safer up there, plus better access to restrooms."

Daniella stopped and placed a supporting hand on Luca's chest as she leaned in close to his ear to shout above the deafening noise. "I have over a month yet and I feel fine."

He placed his hand firmly on her hip. "It's not up for negotiation."

She gestured toward the huddle of vendors selling sweet and savory snacks. "We'll miss all the great food."

"We'll get something now and take it with us."

Her eyes had an impish glow and he accepted that as a silent agreement between the pair of them. Enthusiastic partakers and spectators blew whistles and played a variety of percussion instruments. Flags and banners were waved eagerly in unison with the samba beats and sashaying of bodies as they wove their way through the masses.

"One bottle of Brazil's finest water for you, *Senhora*, as requested," he joked, and handed her the bottle purchased from the vendor.

"Thank you. *Viva*!" She lifted her bottle to chink alongside his *caipirinha*.

"So, what do you want to eat?" Luca snaked his arm around Daniella's waist and drew her close to his body.

"Hmm, everything," she teased, pointing to the vendor who was grilling *espetinhos*. "But let's start here." The typical Brazilian snack of barbecued chicken and sausage kebabs smelled delicious as the vendor methodically flipped them across the griddle.

"Funny, I remember these being one of Miguel's favorite foods when we were kids." Her body tensed under his arm as he spoke. "The baby must certainly take after him and have the Venancio genes."

He turned to the vendor and was secretly thankful to be away from her gaze. He wished to hell and back that the baby she was carrying was his and nobody else's. His body tensed at the thought of another man's hands on her, as fury and frustration built inside of him.

"Who says they aren't my favorite?" Her voice was standoffish and her jaw was clenched.

"Because you never used to eat this when we were together. Not once, in fact."

She fidgeted under his gaze, biting her bottom lip. "I've changed my mind. I'm not very hungry—"

"Stop it. What the baby wants, she will have." Luca gave the vendor the money in exchange for two kebabs and handed her one. "Here. Now eat up."

* * * *

Daniella hesitated before accepting the food Luca held out to her. She hated it when he was right. It was true, she had never liked *espetinhos*, but pregnancy had changed a lot of things and her taste buds were one of them. She knew damn well it wasn't physically possible for her growing baby to desire something, and it was even more absurd to think that he or she took after Miguel, so it was down to her change in hormones. Simple as that. But something niggled at the back of her mind, eating away at her as she stared down at the food in her hand.

What if her baby was like its father? What if he or she was more like Miguel than her? What if she couldn't love her child? What if… Panic gripped her throat as the questions consumed her. *Stop analyzing things.*

She was right—not Luca. Pushing his comment aside, she decided to only listen to herself. It was just a piece of chicken, after all, nothing more and nothing less. It was not going to determine anything about her child and its personality.

"Come on, let's move now that you're fed and watered." A smile spread its way across his mouth. It was infectious and she couldn't stop her lips from mirroring his boyish grin.

Luca kept an iron grip on her hand as he pushed through the crowds and guided them toward the *camarotes*. A gentleman in the carnival staff uniform greeted them, nodded to Luca, and automatically opened the door without checking their tickets.

"Sir, we will be outside," a voice called behind them.

Daniella looked over her shoulder and saw Luca shaking hands in turn with four heavily built and armed men. Bodyguards?

The attendee closed the door behind them, leaving them alone in the suite, which could easily fit another twenty guests. The *camarote* offered a perfect, eye level view of the parade, access to one's own bar and readily prepared buffet, plus first class waiter service.

She rolled her eyes. "Bodyguards, really?"

"You won't tell me why you fear for your life–sorry, my life–so I improvised. I told you it would be safe, didn't I?" Luca's hand rested on the small of her back and worked tiny, affectionate circles through the fabric of her dress.

"Hmm," she responded, leaning into him.

The noise was incredible and the atmosphere crackled with electricity from the crowd's excitement and passion. The hypnotic samba rhythms and thunderous drumbeats pulsated through the whole of Rio and filled everybody with the joy of life. Flamboyantly colored outfits clung to both men and women as they twirled and strutted along the procession. Countless glitzy sequins and enormous tropical colored feathers finished off the remarkable attention to detail of the dancer's outfits. Costumes had flares of originality and competition, some the most scant and sparing of material just covering the wearer's modesty.

"This is very cool, I have to admit," Daniella said.

Luca collected two drinks from the barman and offered her a fresh orange juice, which she accepted, keeping her gaze on the never ending stretch of color and sounds.

"I told you. Now are you going to dance with me or what?"

A high-pitched shriek type giggle escaped her as he

grabbed hold of her free hand and pulled her to him; he was already moving in time with the rhythm.

"Check you out," she teased, and naturally followed his lead.

"Well, I have a few moves in my repertoire." He winked.

* * * *

"Thank you for today. It was just what I needed." Daniella looked across the Bentley. Luca was relaxed with one arm resting along the top of the back seat and softly grazing against her neck. The warmth radiated from his fingertips and sent wave after wave of delicious shivers throughout her body.

He faced her and threw her off guard with his dark, penetrating gaze as if he was searching inside of her. "You don't need to thank me, but you're welcome."

It was now late and they had stayed longer than their agreed couple of hours. Luca had anticipated that she would feel tired early on, but she had been the one to pull him up out of his chair for further dances and cheering. Feelings of security, belonging and…love settled comfortably deep within her as she thought back to how his arms had been tightly wrapped around her for the most part of the evening.

"Sir, we're going to take another route. We're being tailed."

Daniella was snatched away from her daydream by the head bodyguard's gruff voice.

What did he just say? Adrenalin began to pump around her body, making her fidget in her seat.

"Fine," Luca calmly replied without moving a muscle.

"What did you just say?" Daniella needed no repetition, but still the words stumbled out of her mouth. "We're being followed, by who?"

The bodyguard looked over his shoulder at her and then to Luca, as if seeking permission to expose whom their followers were. Luca raised his eyebrows in a nonchalant fashion.

"They appear to be *favela* folk, Miss. All male. It's all in hand and nothing for you to worry about."

She knew he was lying. He might be professionally trained to lie in an attempt to ease her worry, but Daniella didn't believe a word of it. Worrying was something she'd been doing for a long time, and she wasn't about to stop now. Especially when it came to the gang. The air was sucked from her lungs and she clutched her stomach as her brain processed his words.

Regulating her breathing had suddenly become the most challenging thing in the world as her mouth dried and her stomach knotted with anxiety.

"See, this is exactly what I meant earlier. You don't…know what they are capable of—"

"Stop the car," Luca interrupted, still remaining in the same poised and calm position.

"Sir?" The chauffeur made eye contact with him in the rearview mirror, one eyebrow raised in question.

"I said stop the car, pull over."

"What are you doing? Are you mad? You just heard what he said, they are from Miguel's gang and—"

Luca rested his index finger on her lips to prevent her from speaking. "You need to remember they were my gang long before Miguel's. I just need five minutes with them and this will all be forgotten. You won't need to worry yourself sick anymore, though God only knows why you do."

"It's not that simple." Daniella licked her lips as he removed his finger. She was aware of the car grinding to a halt on the side of the road. "Please, Luca, I'm begging you. Don't…you don't know what they're capable of…" She held firmly on to his forearm, attempting to anchor him to the spot.

"*Querida*, you really think so naively of me?" His face was relaxed and his voice was full of confidence. Removing her hand from his arm, he then placed a tender kiss across her knuckles. "Wait here and don't move. I'll be right back, I promise." His gaze lowered to her pregnant abdomen before he released her trembling hand and opened the car door.

She watched as the bodyguard also exited.

No. No, I can't let him.

"Luca!" She threw open the door and closed the space between them.

"I told you to stay put." Luca growled at her, the first sign of his relaxed face tensing.

"I couldn't…I can't…I'm scared." Her body shook and she wished his arms were enveloping her safely as they had done earlier that evening.

"You have nothing to be scared of, Daniella." He looked up and then back at her. "I swear to God, I will let nothing happen to you or your baby."

One car and three motorbikes came to loud standstill a few meters ahead of them. Daniella reluctantly lifted her gaze to follow Luca's, which was fixed on one man at the front of the group. A man in his early twenties, muscular, with an arrogant stance and the telltale gang tattoo on his neck. Her gaze moved back to Luca's neck and again registered the slightly scarred area. An inkling of reassurance warmed her knowing he'd had the tattoo removed and was no longer part of their ruthless family.

Were they there to harm Luca? Would they hurt him…kill him? Were they still following Miguel's orders even though he was no longer there? She swallowed the bile that had risen in her throat as if it were razor blades. She couldn't let him go alone.

"But it's not me I'm worried for," she whispered into his chest.

His hand supported the back of her head as his fingers entangled amongst her curls, softly massaging her scalp. "I have told you before, you don't need to worry about me."

"But I do. You're not meant to be here and if they…" She pushed her face harder into his body and inhaled his cologne, the masculine scent that was all him.

She wasn't making sense to herself let alone to Luca. She couldn't tell him the truth. She had always worried about him; from the very second Miguel had threatened his life with his vicious words. She knew that

Luca's twisted younger sibling was capable of staying true to his word to fulfill his spiteful plan of jealousy and blackmail. Even after Luca left Brazil, she had worried about his safety. Had they followed him? Had Miguel lied to her and continued to threaten his brother's life even after her sacrifice? She'd spent so much time worrying that it now even filled her dreams, her nightmares, on a regular basis.

"Trust me, okay?" His free hand cupped her chin and forced her to look up at him, to meet his intense gaze that ignited heat deep within her belly. His eyes watched her with such intensity it made her feel dizzy. "*Sim?*"

She caught her bottom lip between her teeth and bit down hard enough to taste her own blood.

"Stop doing that." His thumb brushed over her bottom lip. "You need to trust me."

* * * *

Daniella's nails dug into Luca's hand as they closed the space between them and the group of men. She had insisted on going with him and had been on the brink of hysteria when he'd said no. With her nails sinking into his flesh, he questioned why she was so scared of the familiar men now standing before them.

"Ricardo." Luca nodded his head to casually greet the man obviously now in charge.

Ricardo inhaled the last drag from his cigarette, dropped it to the pavement, and used the heel of his shoe to put it out. He was in his early twenties and Luca clearly remembered him as a kid. Now, several years later, there he was, attempting to intimidate by folding his arms across his chest, just enough to reveal a glimpse of the gun tucked into the side of his waistband.

"You're not welcome in Brazil." Finally Ricardo spoke, his gaze darting from Daniella back to Luca.

"Well, I had some business to attend to." *Yes, business,* he reminded himself. *Remember. Treat her like a business plan.* "And naturally I wanted to pay my respects to my brother."

Ricardo grimaced at Luca's last words. "Miguel would turn in his grave knowing you were here. How long do you intend to stay?"

Luca shrugged and kept his gaze firmly on Ricardo. "Like I said, I'm here for business. Once it's finished, I will be gone."

Daniella's nails withdrew one by one, and she wriggled her fingers in his palm as she fidgeted beside him and he instantly knew what she was thinking.

What about her?

Ricardo's gaze shifted and fell on their joined hands, and he raised an eyebrow. "And you think your brother would be pleased about this? Taking his wife and child? And you…" He looked Daniella up and down and snorted. "You didn't wait long before running back and shacking up with him, did you?"

"Hey! You're talking to me, not her." Luca's voice boomed and filled the silent night all around them. Lunging forward, he dropped Daniella's hand and was nose to nose with Ricardo. The adrenalin surged through his body and he was ready to protect what was his now. His fighting days were long over, but he could still fight if necessary.

Ricardo and the other five men scowled and retreated slightly. Their apparent bravado and attitude vanished within seconds.

"Don't be a fool and outstay your welcome, Venancio. We wouldn't want this to end…unnecessarily, would we? I don't want your blood on my hands, but equally, I don't want you in Brazil. Finish your business and then leave. You're not welcome here. You lost the right to be here when you deserted your family."

Luca knew Ricardo was referring to the gang as his

family. He'd walked years ago and ultimately signed his farewell to Brazil. He'd left the gang in his teenage years, but remained living and working in Rio, a silent agreement reached between him and the rest of them.

Luca leaned forward and whispered into Ricardo's ear so nobody else could catch what he said. "You wouldn't have it in you, kid. You should know by now, I do not take orders from anyone, especially my little brother and his errand boys. I ran things long before you could even walk, and whatever my reasons were for leaving the family, they're none of your fucking business. Now run along."

Ricardo stared back at him, but quickly looked away. Luca admitted that Ricardo was good at the 'imitating bad guy' act, but deep down inside he didn't have the gumption to follow through with his threats. Although they may hate him, he knew the majority of the men still held some form of respect for their previous leader.

Ricardo muttered something and the group of men followed him back to their vehicles.

"What just happened? What did you say?" Daniella was behind him with one trembling hand on his forearm.

Cupping her face with both hands, he bent down to

meet her lips.

Business, Luca. She's just business.

Chapter 8

Luca looked into the large mirror on the bathroom wall and fixed the knot of his bow tie. He knew he had nothing to worry about with regard to the gala this evening. After hiring a successful event planner to deal with the details, he knew it would run like clockwork.

He'd showered and dressed in his tailor-made tuxedo, all the while thinking how sweet his revenge would taste.

It would be tonight. She was head over heels in love with him, again, and now all he had to do was take what he wanted and end it. *Simple.*

He caught his reflection in the mirror and his gaze fell upon the frown lines on his forehead. For the briefest of seconds, he barely recognized the man staring back at him. Could he be so cold, so cruel? It was simple…wasn't it?

He dragged one hand over his face and met his reflection once again. He raised his eyebrows and then closed his eyes in an attempt to get rid of the lines and the uncomfortable feelings of guilt within him. He buttoned up the tux jacket and took one last look in the mirror. *Business.*

Luca made his way to the lounge and poured himself a generous measure of expensive whiskey while he waited for Daniella. His mind conjured up images of how she would look…what would she be wearing, how would she smell? Although she'd argued several times that she didn't want him to spend money on her, he'd won the fight and insisted her dress be tailor-made and that he would be paying. End of discussion. He'd hired the best couturier this side of the globe, knowing she would create something suitable for Daniella and the gala scene. She had to look the part, although to him she would look stunning draped in a rubbish bag. Her natural beauty shone through whatever she wore.

The soft click of heels interrupted his thoughts and he turned. Daniella was standing at the top of the twisting marble staircase. Luca was aware of his jaw dropping as he took in the vision before him. Her long, chocolate-colored curls were styled and loosely cascaded over her shoulders. Her petite figure was wrapped in a rich, two-tone, floor-sweeping gown; a deep azure blue silk covered the top half of her body with a plunging V-neck and short, kimono-style sleeves barely skimmed the top of her arms. A block of indigo blue fell and draped from under her bust to the floor, elegantly swathing over her small, neat baby bump.

She slowly descended the staircase, clutching her evening purse with one hand and the stair rail with the other. Luca threw back the last mouthful of whiskey and moved closer to the bottom step and offered her his hand.

A faint smile spread across her lips when she placed her soft hand in his palm.

"You look…" He shook his head, utterly lost for words. The most flattering wouldn't have been enough to describe the image in front of him. For a split second, he worried he was about to lose control. She was a vision of beauty.

"I know, I know. I'm sure I look like a whale," Daniella finished his sentence for him.

"*Ridiculo*," he protested and helped her off the final step. "You look like a goddess. I have never seen anything more exquisite in my life."

His pulse quickened; she was how he imagined perfection would look. Flawless and breathtaking in every sense of the word. Her golden-colored skin shone with a vitality he'd never noticed before. As each day passed, she appeared healthier and she glowed with a luminescent beauty. Pregnancy suited her and enhanced her womanliness.

"There is something missing. Wait one minute." He turned and left her standing alone whilst he collected a small designer box from his desk.

"Here." He handed her the ribbon-tied box.

"What is it?" she asked, eyeing him and then the box curiously.

"Well, open it and you will see."

"I told you I didn't want any more gifts—"

"Please, just open it. Humor me." He placed his hand on the small of her back. The back of the dress plunged halfway down her spine, leaving bare skin against his fingertips. The feel of her naked flesh against his palm instantly aroused him, battling with his libido.

"Fine, okay." Daniella rolled her eyes and began to undo the ribbon around the black velvet trinket box.

He knew she hated receiving gifts from him. She'd explained enough times that she didn't want to be showered with his money and wanted to earn her own way, which she had been doing through her share of home cooking, much to Maria's disapproval. Wondering why she detested it so much, he found himself asking if perhaps Miguel had not shown her such tenderness and gestures of love.

Love? He took that word back instantly. It was a simple facade of love. As far as he cared, she could throw the jewelry in the trash bin or sell it after he was done with her.

"Oh, Luca." Her soft whisper hung in the air, and he was tugged away from his thoughts yet again.

"I hoped you would like it."

"I love it. It's gorgeous." She lightly ran her fingers over the set of delicate diamond and gold-leaf necklace and earrings. "You shouldn't have—"

"Hush. Now try it on." He took the necklace from the box and fastened the intricate chain around her neck.

Daniella set the box on a nearby coffee table and fastened the earrings before he held both of her hands and stood back to admire her once more.

"Breathtaking."

A rosy-colored glow shone in her cheeks as if he'd embarrassed her.

"Let's go." He offered her his arm. "Tonight, all of Rio will see just how beautiful you are."

Daniella accepted his gesture and slid her arm through his. Out of the corner of his eye, Luca watched her place her hand to her bump and give a gentle, almost reassuring touch. Yet again he was reminded of the innocent child between them as guilt tugged at his heart.

* * * *

The limousine came to a gentle standstill outside their destination and Daniella sank into her seat. Her stomach was fluttering uncontrollably with nerves, along with some vigorous kicks from her baby. She wasn't sure she could go through with this. She was the type of person who liked to stay well and truly out of the limelight, safely tucked away in her own world—to blend in with everyday life and not cause a scene. She had learned quickly not to question or talk back to Miguel and his gang, for fear of the consequences and actions that would meet her. Drawing attention to herself wasn't a good thing and often left her a target for his temper.

You never used to be like that.

This wasn't the time—nor the place—for her subconscious to start talking to her.

Tonight, this would be another world, a world of which she knew nothing. It was Luca's circle and she needed him more than ever to get through it. She'd reluctantly agreed to be his guest and continued to reassure herself it was just for a few hours. It wouldn't kill her.

The uniformed concierge opened her door of the sleek black limousine and welcomed her with a warm smile as he extended a hand to her. "*Senhora, boa noite*."

She was on display to the world and his friend and judging gazes would be on her as soon as she stepped inside of the building.

The off-white, almost cream-colored building caught her eye as she quickly thanked the man. It was stunning. She knew exactly where she was, instantly recognizing the magnificent architecture and its 1920's art deco style, but still her eyes gravitated toward the sign above the entrance. *Copacabana Palace.*

The palace was actually a hotel, and one of Rio's finest. She knew it attracted some of the top A-listers and wealthiest socialites in the world. Rich, beautiful, and elegant folk made up the guest list. What it didn't attract was the ordinary person like her, the widow of a twisted criminal who was now eight months pregnant and without a cent to her name. The Copacabana Palace did not make a habit of welcoming her type.

"Relax, you are meant to be enjoying yourself." Luca was beside her again, squeezing her hand and placing a soft kiss on the back of it.

"I really don't belong here." There were bound to be hundreds of extremely wealthy men and women present, all discussing business and their bank accounts whilst blatantly judging one another. Sheer panic took hold of her, closing tightly around her throat, and her hand trembled under his strong grip.

"Who says so? You are with me. You are my guest, and I say who does and who does not attend."

"People are going to gossip. They're going to ask who I am, and when they find out I'm just your sister-in-law, they—"

"*Parà-lo!*"

He stopped and faced her square on and looked down into her eyes. He'd created that magnetic hold over her once more, the same as he had back in her dingy kitchen the day of Miguel's funeral. The day he had finally come back into her life. *Damn, how did he do it?*

"You know you will always be more than just that to me." Luca touched the loose curl beside her cheek. Tucking it behind her ear, he whispered, "You always have been."

Daniella released the breath she'd been holding and

felt her muscles relax. His breath on her neck sent a shiver down her spine and goose bumps rose on her arms. The evening air was humid and warm; she had no reason to be shivering. She knew it was his hot breath and masculine cologne teasing her senses and making her giddy.

Luca's gaze traveled across her face, down her neck, and over the swell of her breasts. He frowned and traced a finger down the same trail and outlined her breast. Leaning in close to her, he firmly placed his hand just above her buttocks. "Tonight I will have you, Daniella."

His words fired hot sparks of electricity through her as if lighting a switch for the first time. There was confidence in his tone, a certainty she had never witnessed until now. Was she ready for this to happen? She'd asked for time, and he'd patiently given her just that.

Of course you want it! Her subconscious rudely overrode her thoughts. *Just a few days ago you wanted him in the back of his car. Stop lying to yourself. Denying yourself.*

She was right.

Of course I'm right!

Before she could organize her thoughts and stop the crazy dialogue in her head, Luca had hold of her hand and was leading her up half a dozen steps.

His words echoed in her head as she let herself be chaperoned by his hands. *Tonight I will have you.*

* * * *

A sexual hunger surged through Luca at full speed as he took Daniella's hand and led her toward the hotel's entrance. He needed to have her now, take her body and use it however he wanted, but the gala was in the way of taking what was rightfully his.

As they approached the glass doors, two gentlemen immediately opened them.

"*Boa noite, Senhor e senhora.*" One of the men welcomed them as they walked through the doorway.

Daniella's heels clicked against the aesthetic marble flooring as she kept up with his strides. *Slow down, the woman is near to giving birth!*

He cast a sideways glance at her and sucked in a breath—he wasn't sure he could wait the entire evening. Part of him wanted to take her there and then in the hallway, not having a care in the world about who was nearby. Her eyes were opened wide—hesitant and nervous, like a deer caught in the headlights—her emerald green irises looked up at him. Before he could question the emotion he thought he'd seen, a woman serving slim flutes of champagne approached them.

"Good evening, *Senhor Venancio e Senhora*." Her eye contact was solely on Luca as she greeted them both and offered a crystal flute of the expensive, honey-colored liquid laced with tiny bubbles.

Luca reached for two glasses, one of which had a golden rim. He extended the unique, standalone glass to Daniella.

"You know I can't drink alcohol." She smiled and raised her hand in front of her.

"See the gold rim? They had this specially made for my guest." He held the flute close to her fingertips and waited for her to accept. "You don't need to worry, it's non-alcoholic."

Daniella took the crystal from him, and bewilderment and inquisitiveness crossed her face as she raised it to her lips.

"Thank you." She beamed at him and took a sip.

"You are very welcome."

"The last time I had real champagne was with…" Her words stopped short.

"With who? Miguel?" Luca inquired softly.

He watched as the curves of her smile slowly faded. "Oh no, I don't think Miguel even knew what champagne was."

"So, who was it with?"

Luca kept his gaze fixed on her face, watching the anxious bite of her lips and the slight rosy glow spread across her cheeks. She slowly tilted her head to look up at him again, her long, dark eyelashes framing her eyes.

Did she realize just how expressive her eyes were? The bite of her lip, the blushing…

Having both a Brazilian and an American parent had given her the most perfectly complimentary features and they still managed to captivate him as if it was the first time he was meeting her.

"It was with you…on our engagement."

Luca reminisced back to their short, but intense, eight months together and clearly recalled the occasion Daniella was referring to. How could he forget? The night he'd proposed at the peak on Sugarloaf Mountain, all of Rio's spectacular scenery as their witness whilst he presented her with an intricately patterned platinum band, iced with a square, polished diamond. Inside he'd had the words *Always thankful for faulty bags and runaway oranges. All my love. L.* inscribed around the inner rim of the precious metal. They'd toasted alone at a small and intimate restaurant at the base of the *Pao de Acucar* and embraced their wedded future with fine Dom Perignon champagne.

"I remember." He stared down at her, unblinking as the images resonated in his mind. The ring had shone on her finger, as delicate and precious as her. He coughed to clear his throat and to break the intense picture forming in his mind. "What happened to the ring?

He knew perfectly well what had happened, but probed for her side of the story. The private investigator he'd hired the day after Daniella had walked away from him reported back that he'd witnessed Miguel snatching the ring from her finger and entering a pawnbroker's store. Luca had transferred sufficient funds to his PI and demanded he wasn't to leave the brokers until that ring was safely in his pocket. Days later, Luca had met with him to be handed the ring, which had since lain safely in his office vault in New York. He wasn't entirely sure why he'd gone to extreme measures to ensure the possession of the ring. *Because you love her, you fool.*

Daniella ran her fingertip along the rim of the crystal flute. "Miguel pawned it."

"For what in return?"

"You really want to know?"

"Probably not." He shrugged.

She took a sip of the fruity liquid before she answered. "He made a nice profit on it, but it was soon wasted on drugs, alcohol, weapons, things like that."

Luca closed his eyes for a second and then opened them, meeting with her pained look. Her glow had faded and sadness filled her eyes. He pushed the memories as far away as possible and squeezed her hand. "Come, let's go in. But on this occasion you have to stick to just non-alcoholic fruit infused champagne, *querida*." He shot her a tight smile and then led her further into the hotel.

A set of grand oak doors were opened ahead of them in anticipation and revealed a tasteful and elegant room. Soft musical tones filled the atmosphere with a relax-and-unwind vibe.

"Welcome to the Copacabana Piano Bar, *Senhor* Venancio." The manager of the bar extended his hand to Luca.

He accepted the man's welcome gesture and pulled Daniella slightly closer toward him.

"For now, please enjoy the reception cocktails and aperitifs. You may start to make your way to Antique

Casino Room at nine o'clock for the banquet and entertainment."

The event planner had surpassed her task tenfold. The soft glow of the bar's lighting illumed the aqua blue pool outside and the subtle, jazzy beats of the pianist filled Luca with an edge of excitement.

The room was filled with over three hundred guests, all pleasantly pretending to socialize with each other. The class in which he now moved was a ball game of its own. It was dog-eat-dog and he had to remain top of the pack. It was funny how his present lifestyle mirrored the behaviors of his *favela* years.

"Oh, I can't do this." Daniella tried to pull her hand away, but he had a firm hold.

He could almost see her heart pounding in her chest, the soft silky fabric of her dress ever so slightly vibrating against her skin with each breath. His eyes were intently on hers, which were darting between him and the now wide open doorway ahead.

Luca was used to such environments, elaborate events where all eyes were on him, but she wasn't, not even in the slightest. Even when they had been together before, she hadn't attended anything like this. Most of the invited guests who attended had a disposition to begin the evening with sober business-related chitchat and progress to alcohol-fuelled garbage, Luca thought to himself. Over the years, he had built up a thick skin, resilient to dealing with the rich and pompous. He knew what it was like to be a regular penny in the pocket boy and never forgot the tough streets where he'd come from; it was his being. It ran through his blood like the air he breathed.

"Yes, you can. I want you here with me and nobody else."

It was partly true, he consoled himself. He knew it would turn the evening into a game of Chinese whispers for his guests, but he found himself not bothered.

What was new?

He regularly made the front cover of the New York magazines and papers with different women on his arm. They would believe Daniella to be just another victim of his charm and bed. Yet, a natural, warm sensation surged through him and he knew that could never be the case with Daniella. She had always been his world.

Swallowing hard, as if tasting something foul, he remembered this was not part of the plan, for him at least. His boundaries were crossing and he needed to remain focused. He had to stay determined, stay cold inside, but it was difficult because she meant more to him than any other woman ever could. Flurries of guilt rose from the pit of his stomach again. Could he go through with this plan?

Get a grip. Remember what she did to you. What they both did to you, Miguel and Daniella.

Pushing the memories to the back of his mind, he forced a smile and said, “I promise I won’t leave your side.”

Chapter 9

Daniella entwined her fingers even tighter into Luca's already strong hold, praying he wouldn't let go of her for fear of falling to the floor and embarrassing both of them. Her legs were quivering like jelly, and the damn heels, even though they were only two inches high, were not helping with her balance. She had enough to concentrate on with making eye contact, smiling, and trying to suck in her impressive baby bump, let alone worrying about keeping her balance.

Damn, why hadn't she worn flats? Flats would have given her one less thing to—

"Luca. Splendid location. What made you change from the usual?"

Daniella cautiously raised her head and her gaze settled on the middle-aged man who had interrupted her thoughts. A twenty-something-year-old girl clung to his arm, and his face displayed a self-righteous arrogance. He extended his free hand toward Luca who accepted it with a firm shake.

"Marcus, how are you, old friend?" His greeting of an obvious business associate was pleasant. "I thought it was about time people had a taste of my birthplace, and besides, what is there not to like about Brazil?"

"Less of the 'old', please," replied the graying man as he cast another curious glance from Luca to her. "And who might you be, Miss?"

Luca's gaze flicked from Marcus's face to her pregnant belly and then back to his guest, and Daniella placed a protective hand over her bump. She knew Luca had changed his whole annual gala arrangements for her. Her alone.

He knew she couldn't fly being so far into her pregnancy, so he'd invited his associates to wine and dine in Rio de Janeiro—one of the most vibrant cities in the world.

Daniella wanted to jump behind Luca and cling on to him for dear life. She hated everything about this environment—the pomposity, the arrogance, the two-faced façade, and much more. She leaned against Luca for support.

"I…I'm…" She stumbled over her words and her mind went blank as fear grabbed at her throat.

"Please, let me. This is Ms. Daniella Marie Venancio."

She exhaled quickly. Luca had rescued her with his

effortless conversation and demeanor. It was another action which showed his ease within the high flying circle of socialites. Marcus reached for Daniella's hand and placed a small kiss on the back of it.

Smiling through gritted teeth, she wondered if she should introduce herself properly, explain who she really was. "I'm Luca's—"

"Honorary guest." He swiftly cut off her explanation and took her hand in his. He rubbed the back of it gently with the pad of his thumb, his gaze fixed heavily on hers for a moment before he looked back to Marcus.

She bit her lip and took the hint to keep her explanations to herself. Was Luca embarrassed about who she really was? Heat flamed her cheeks and all she could do was nod in Marcus's direction.

"It's a pleasure to meet you," she said.

"No, Ms. Venancio, the pleasure is certainly all mine."

Daniella heard the slight emphasis on her name, as if he was purposely drawing attention to her married surname and silently questioning who and where her husband was. His steel-gray eyes flicked over her midriff and back to Luca. He tilted one eyebrow quizzically and opened his mouth as if ready to ask questions, but was brought to a halt by the young woman who hung off his arm. She was starting to get fidgety.

"I need another drink," she whined.

The couple departed and Marcus threw a last curious glance over his shoulder.

"Are you embarrassed by me?" Daniella couldn't stop the words from tumbling out of her mouth.

"*Que?* No! Of course not." Luca dropped her hand and snaked his arm around her waist, pulling her closer. "Why on earth do you say that?"

"Why couldn't you tell him who I really am…who we both are?" She acknowledged the round tummy between them.

"For one thing, I don't think it is anyone else's business apart from ours."

"And the second thing?"

"Secondly, I don't want to have to introduce you as my sister-in-law nor my ex-fiancée. I want to be able to announce you as my wife," Luca replied calmly, placing a finger under her chin and turning her to face him.

Adrenalin and exhilaration flooded through her veins and the anxiety that had been knotting in her stomach since leaving home was replaced with excitement.

Was he going to propose? Was he for real? Of course he was, why on earth would he lie?

His hooded, moody eyes held hers in a hypnotic thrall and made her stomach flutter. His mocha-colored skin was smooth-shaven and clear, his jet-black hair and long lashes contributed to a face which could have graced the cover of a fashion magazine.

Her love for him intensified each day. There was no more room inside of her to suppress her feelings, desires. Her heart physically ached as she tried to break away from him. *I love you. I always have.*

Daniella was suddenly aware of her dry throat and it was difficult to swallow. She lifted the personalized flute to her lips and sipped at the liquid. The fruity mix of papaya and lime soothed her parched throat.

"Daniella."

"*Monsieur* Venancio…" A male voice interrupted their private and intense moment, and before she could say anything, Luca was initiating further handshakes.

Luca maneuvered her around the room, almost in succession with the pianist's flawless playing, and shook each gentleman's hand firmly and placed one kiss on each of the female guests' cheeks, but there was minimal sincerity in his greetings. It appeared even the gala, which was organized to bring together businessmen and women alike to socialize, was still a highly structured game within itself. The look-down-the-nose etiquette was false, and Daniella knew as soon as they turned away, the backstabbing conversations would begin.

Luca let go of her hand and placed his on the small of her back, letting her know he was right behind her. The heat radiated from his palm through the thin silk of her dress and she was sure it seared a burning red mark on her skin.

As the gala got underway, she had to admit she was enjoying herself. Although the company wasn't her first choice, the cuisine and the glamorous venue were incredible. As was the constant touch and attention from Luca.

The 1920's art deco and fine décor created an ambience as though they had stepped back in time to the decade of Hollywood glamour, rubbing shoulders with past and present A-listers. She devoured her appetizer Caesar salad, and main course of *Picadinho Copacabana* along with all of its side dishes. Although, glancing around her table, she noticed that the majority of female guests left the food after pushing it around the plate.

Luca leaned over and whispered into her ear. “Let’s go home. I’m done here.”

“But we haven’t been here very long.”

“I’ve greeted everyone and now I want to leave. With you,” he explained as he downed his last mouthful of champagne.

“They haven’t even brought out the dessert yet.”

He traced a finger along her jaw line and stopped at the corner of her lips. She remembered his words at the beginning of the night. *Tonight I will have you, Daniella.*

One eyebrow was raised and a mischievous glint shone wickedly in his eyes which were ablaze. “I can certainly provide dessert.”

Daniella bit down on her lip to stifle the giggle inside of her. The double meaning of his statement caused her to shiver with excitement.

“Come on, let’s get out of here.” They stood and he took her hand, tucking it into his arm.

“Mr. Venancio.” A man’s voice called Luca from behind. “I would like to have a word with you.”

“I’m leaving now, but you can contact my secretary to arrange a convenient time of us both.” Luca turned to face the Saudi businessman.

“I think you will be very interested in what I have

to say about a possible third contract. Handsome figures."

Luca's eyes met with his opponent and Daniella knew he was back in the business frame of mind.

"Why don't we have a quick nightcap?" the man asked. He looked over Luca's shoulder, his eyes trailing up and down Daniella. "Alone."

She gripped tighter on to Luca's forearm.

Luca hesitated for a moment before turning to Daniella. "Wait here. I will only be five minutes."

"But you promised you wouldn't leave me," she whispered.

He leaned in to whisper in her ear. "This man is one of the biggest catches, I just need a couple of minutes. I won't be far." Luca pried himself away from her grip and shook the man's hand before leading him to the bar area.

Daniella sat alone at one of the vacant chairs, hoping she would blend into the background like a wallflower. *Fine chance!*

"So *you* are the new fancy bit?" A high-pitched, matter-of-fact voice came from behind her.

"Excuse me?" Daniella turned to face the woman and her gaze fell upon a leggy, size zero blonde who stood with her hands on her hips.

"You are Luca's new toy I presume?" she repeated.

Daniella smiled to herself, unsure how to interpret the observation.

"Sorry, who are you?" She gripped the edge of the chair as she looked into the woman's icy, blue eyes.

The woman stepped closer toward her. "I am the only one who could satisfy Luca, and by the looks of things, I still am." She ran her eyes across Daniella's tummy and snorted. "That—" She pointed her long, manicured finger at Daniella's unborn child. "—is clearly not his." Her strong French accent accentuated the cruel words, and they were like a slap across the face.

Daniella opened and closed her mouth as her brain processed the vicious words.

"Luca did not want any children. He said they would hold him back from his career and were too much hassle." The blonde stepped closer so she was just inches away. "That's why we always used protection. Something you obviously know nothing about, you silly little girl. I understand Luca in every single way possible. We are two of a kind. What could you possibly offer him?"

The woman's cold and judgmental eyes were locked firmly on Daniella's and her lips were set in a petulant pout. Images of this vindictive creature and Luca, her hero, her only love, began to cloud her mind. She knew he had been with women during her marriage to Miguel; she wasn't silly or naive by any means, but the thought of him being with a woman like the one standing before her churned her stomach.

Standing as tall as possible to match her accuser, adrenaline surged through Daniella's veins like power igniting her tired body. For a moment, her legs trembled and threatened to collapse beneath her. She'd experienced enough abuse and humiliation over the years and she was not going to allow herself to be treated that way again. Ever. By anyone. Especially this jealous ex!

Who did this woman think she was? It was fight-or-flight and her mind and body had chosen to fight.

Daniella was several inches shorter than the leggy blonde, but it didn't faze her. She wanted to inform her that Luca did not care for bleached blonde and fake tanned women, but instead she refrained and kept her composure.

"The name of my baby's father is Venancio."

Daniella collected her bag. “Now if you’ll excuse me.”

“Wait a minute, you little home wrecker.” The woman grabbed at Daniella’s wrist.

“Get your hands off of me.” Daniella’s voice rose and guests turned and stared.

“When he comes to his senses, he’ll throw you and that bastard child on to the streets where you belong, and he will come straight back to me.” Her words cut through Daniella like an ice-cold dagger to her heart.

She looked over the woman’s shoulder and saw Luca sipping from a large tumbler glass as he nodded along with what his associate had to say. Could he have really been interested in this cruel woman, have been intimate and loving with her? Her mind raced. It seemed ludicrous, but had he changed so much over the last several years that she didn’t know him anymore? Her eyes fell on the woman’s scrawny fingers.

“Please remove your hand or I will call for security to remove you.”

One by one the nearby guests fell silent and watched.

“Stupid little girl.” The woman released her hold, allowing Daniella to leave.

She had to get out of that place, with or without

Luca. Her heels clicked against the marble floor as she hurried across the never-ending room. Nausea threatened to consume her, and she needed fresh air. She pushed the set of exit of doors open, almost knocking down the concierges.

"*Senhora,* is everything okay?" one of the men asked. "Shall I send for *Senhor* Venancio?"

Daniella covered her mouth with one hand and tried to hold back the pricking of tears that pushed to be released. The other hand she held out in front of her, signaling she was all right.

"I'm fine." It took all of her control to keep her voice from betraying her. "I'm fine. I would just like to go home now."

"Of course, right away." The concierge summonsed a limousine waiting nearby with a flick of his hand.

Daniella fell into the luxury car and rested her head against the back of the leather seat. The driver was a member of Luca's chauffeur staff and didn't require directions, giving her time to close her eyes and be alone.

She didn't know whether to believe what the blonde had told her or just put it down to jealous lies, but she knew she didn't want to meet the woman and her cruel tongue again.

* * * *

"Daniella?" Luca flung open the front door and then paced from room to room, continuing to shout for her, his voice booming through each room as he entered. "Daniella?"

He'd checked all of the ground floor rooms and there was no sign of her. Was she okay?

Dread filled him to the pit of his stomach. The hotel staff had informed him she had left in a provided limousine and was driven by his regular staff, but had they physically taken her into the property and ensured she was safe? Damn it! Why hadn't she just waited for him?

"Daniella?"

He climbed the stairs two at a time as an energy surged through him. Shrouded in darkness at the top of the landing, the light shone beneath the door of the guest room.

Daniella's room.

The light crept from the edge of the closed door and toward him, beckoning him closer. He quickly closed the space, turned the handle, and entered. The feminine patterned bed linen was still made and untouched with

Daniella not in sight. He dragged a hand through his hair and swore to himself before his gaze caught sight of the en suite door that was ajar. His banging heart now pounded in his ears and the surge of adrenalin slowly faded, leaving him with the slightest tremor.

He pushed the door back on its hinges. The huge bathtub was full to the brim with bubbles and Daniella lay back in the bath, her nose out of the water and the rest of her face submerged. Eyes closed, her dark lashes rested on the tops of her cheeks and her hair floated about her shoulders with a sense of serenity. The floral scent of the bubble bath filled his nostrils and reminded him to control his ragged breath now that he'd found her. He dragged both hands over his face as relief washed over him. Was he thankful she was safe or that she was still there?

Luca shrugged out of his tux jacket and released the top button of his shirt, leaving the bow tie hanging loosely around his neck. He placed his hands into his trouser pockets and hesitated—he didn't want to frighten her so he moved slowly to close the space between him and the tub. The mountain of soapy suds covered every part of her body apart from the tops of her shoulders and head, leaving the rest to his imagination and a few memories.

Crouching down onto his haunches, he rested his elbows on his knees and brought both hands together under his chin. His gaze wandered the length of the bath, of her hidden body, and settled upon her eyes. Of course he'd been worried about her safety. It was only natural to feel like that. So how was he going to feel come tomorrow morning when he was saying goodbye for the last time?

Daniella's movement distracted him from his inner torment. She lifted her head and pushed herself up so that her shoulders and back rested against the slope of the bath. Her dark wet hair, now deadly straight without a curl in sight, was slick and molded to her shoulders. Her lips were slightly parted, full and pouty, ready to be kissed. She opened her eyes and met his gaze with a look of intensity.

"Why did you leave? They told me you were going home. I told you to wait for me, I thought you…the baby…" Although he'd regained his composure, his words were jumbled and he sounded like a mad man.

"I didn't really want to stay around and be spoken to like rubbish. I knew you were busy, so I came home. You can see we are safe."

"I see." He rose to his feet and sat on the edge of the bath.

"Do you mind? I'm trying to relax and—"

"I saw Natalie Chevalier talking with you."

"Oh, so the witch does have a name?"

"Please, forget anything she said to you. She is poison."

"You admit you do know her then?"

Luca cleared his throat before answering her. "Yes, we dated for a few months, that's all. Nothing more."

Tension lingered in the air and they stared at each other.

"She said you didn't ever want children, is she right?"

"I certainly didn't want children with her." It was true. Natalie had been one of many women he had spent time with. She had meant nothing to him, nothing emotionally. It had been purely physical, as every other woman had been. After the heartbreak he had gone through with Daniella and his brother, he would not let himself feel that way again, to be trapped and ruined at the hand of another woman. Therefore it was easier to just keep things physical—sexual—with no emotional strings attached.

"I asked if you ever wanted children."

"Yes, of course." He paused, his gaze locked with hers. "But only with one person."

She swallowed and a gulp escaped her throat.

"Only ever with you." He finally broke their gaze and looked down at his hands and then back to her. "If that wasn't possible, then no, I never wanted children."

The bubbles started to disperse, breaking away and scattering small islands unevenly around Daniella's body. Patches of skin were visible through the gaps that the bubbles had created, allowing Luca to have a glance. Her long, silky hair passed her shoulders and covered her breasts in an almost mermaid-type style. The curve of her hip and her thigh tantalized him and had him stifling a groan. The roundness of her belly jutted out of the water, with just a few speckled bubbles left on her skin. It was perfectly round, and her skin glistened from the water and soapsuds. Just the faintest sign of one or two stretch marks could be seen across her pregnant abdomen, making her seem more real, more womanly than any other he had been with. Admiring the full curve of her bump suddenly filled him with the desire to touch it.

Ludicrous. Why should he want to feel something

so precious…something so intimate…something that wasn't his. He couldn't find a reason for it.

Breaking the silence, he asked, "May I?" and lifted his right hand to hover just above her tummy.

Daniella hesitated and then nodded. Nervously, he placed his palm at the top of the neat curve and his fingers spread over her tight skin. Luca realized he was holding his breath and released it with a loud *whoosh* sound.

"*O meu Deus!*" His laugh echoed around the tiled bathroom and he was greeted with a swift kick to his hand.

"Feisty one, huh?"

"You most definitely have a footballer in there. One very strong and healthy baby."

Oh God, why isn't it my baby?

Chapter 10

Luca inhaled deeply, trying to keep his composure, which never failed him, not ever, even in the most difficult situations.

But now, seeing Daniella before him, naked, her skin scattered with tiny pearl-like droplets, he knew he was going to lose control at any second. He removed his hand from her stomach and reached toward the cascading wet hair lying over her swollen breast. With two fingers he gently pushed the slick mane aside and around to the side of her arm. He stifled a growl at the glimpse of the light brown circle that encompassed a rose-pink nipple. It instantly peaked under his gaze. Thoughts of taking the dusky bud-like tip between his lips once again flooded his mind, to roll it softly between his teeth and tease it with his tongue. He trailed the back of his two fingers over the curve of her breast and ribs, allowing his eyes to leisurely follow the path of his fingers. The shallow pant that escaped Daniella's lips turned him on even more.

"You have no idea how exquisite you are," he whispered.

He was going to have her tonight, over and over, all night long, and savor every damn second of it. Eager to put his plan into full throttle, he continued to gently follow the curve of her hips and thighs with his hand. She wasn't stopping him and a wicked glint in her eye incited him to continue. His hand moved deeper into the now translucent water as his fingers left her curves and moved toward the dark curls of hair visible at the apex of her thighs. He wanted to be inside her now, this very second, but knew he had to take it slowly. He'd waited long enough and a few more minutes wouldn't kill him. Nothing was going to happen in here. *No.*

Luca wanted her in his bed, where he could see her, touch her, and make her his. Her eyes were ablaze, large emerald green jewels framed by dark lashes gazed up at him. The blood pounded in his loins and pushed against his trousers, aching to seize the jewel that was rightfully his. The prize that was his. The business deal that was going to be sealed. After all, that was all she was, right?

This was what he wanted, to have his revenge and to have his way. This would be the end. Anything else had just been part of his plan, an illusion for her benefit. He needed her out of the bath and in his bed. He bent and lifted her from the bath in one swift movement.

"What are you doing?" Daniella shrieked as she was plucked from the tub.

She clung to him as he carried her out of the bathroom and down the dark hallway. His shirt, now soaked from her wet body, cooled his skin. He turned the handle of his master bedroom door and kicked it open with his foot.

"I told you I would have you tonight." He set her down on his bed.

He bowed his head to kiss her, his arms pinning hers close to her body. She was still, looking up at him with desire beneath her hooded gaze, as the last droplets of water on her naked skin evaporated into the warm air.

He bent closer to her and waited for her move to meet his lips. To see if she wanted this…needed this as much as he did. He would not force her into anything she didn't want, that wasn't his style. If she objected, then he would have to go back to the drawing board and devise a new strategy.

"I love you, Luca," she whispered.

Ouch. Those words he'd wanted to hear for so long now stung his heart. He swallowed and fought to remain in control

"I love you too. Sometimes too much," he said

softly.

Daniella bit down on her lip and reached up to pull the loose bow tie away from his shirt collar.

Damn it. She had no idea what that did to him—normally it would infuriate him. He knew she bit her lip when she was nervous or self-conscious, but right now she had no reason to be, and it was driving him wild with need. He wanted to capture the soft, pink lip between his own lips and devour her.

Eyes are the portals to the soul and lips are the corridors to the mind, he thought.

His tie fell from her fingers to the floor and then she loosened his shirt buttons. The softness of her fingertips brushed his chest and small shocks of pleasure rippled over his skin.

Oh, those hands.

She eased his shirt up and over his shoulders and it crumpled to the ground before she leaned forward and finally met his kiss. Luca reclaimed her mouth as he pushed his lips gently against hers and cupped her face with both of his hands. His tongue made a sweeping search, needing to taste even more of her intoxicating nectar.

He reluctantly lifted his lips from hers and traced

delicate kisses along her neck until he reached her ear. “Relax,” he whispered.

“I can’t. I look awful.” She spoke quietly and tried to cover her body.

“*Ridiculo*! Why do you always think so little of yourself? You need to stop it.” Luca gently pulled her hands from her body. He held her arms out to the sides of her and, his eyes roamed impatiently over her luscious, feminine curves. “You…you are the most beautiful woman I have ever seen. You have no reason to feel uncomfortable in your own skin. Believe me.”

It was true. Daniella was beautiful. He struggled for a word to describe her type of beauty; unearthly, like a goddess. Even heavily pregnant with another man’s child, she was breathtakingly stunning. The extra weight and curves of her belly, hips, and breasts only made him crave her more than ever.

A pang of guilt hit his heart, hard. He worried she would feel worthless with no self-esteem when he’d finished with her and thrown her out of his home. Could he really do that to her? The moment when she had left his arms for Miguel’s came back to him and he firmed his resolve.

Stop thinking. Closing his eyes, he blocked out his

intruding thoughts and captured her lips once more, this time with a savage and fierce need.

* * * *

This was happening.

Daniella's thoughts were jumbled, but pleasantly, as if she had drunk too much wine. It was him. Luca made her feel this way. When he was near her, she lost touch with reality and embraced a whole new world with him alone, fueled by wanton desire and love.

Her palms glided up his bare chest as she traced over his rippling muscles and flat stomach. She broke away from his hot mouth and shuffled closer toward his body and the edge of the bed, eager to be close to him. He stood beside her and towered over her. Small curls of black hair swirled across his chest and down, leading to a dark trail that snaked past his belly button and down under his trouser belt. She reached for the buckle and unfastened the silver clasp. Luca's hand closed tightly around hers and stopped her from going any further.

"No," he growled, but a mischievous smile crossed his lips.

He moved his knee so it was between her thighs and pushed them open.

"Tonight, I am satisfying you, *querida*." His voice

was gruff and huskiness flavored his words as he kicked off his trousers. “Lay back and relax.”

Daniella was sure Luca was used to women only of Natalie Chevalier’s caliber—leggy and polished, like something out of *Vogue* magazine. She had to admit, Natalie had a body to die for. But obviously, Luca only used Natalie when he needed her.

Daniella wished the dimmed lights were off and the dark hid her from his gaze. *Stop it. Luca isn’t Miguel! When will you see that?*

“Stop thinking.” He was above her and resting on one elbow. With the other hand he gently tapped her temple. “You still don’t believe me, do you? When I look at you, naked or clothed, all I see is perfection. Complete and utter perfection.”

Daniella rested back against the luxurious cushions and relished the touch of the silk sheets against her skin. His words rang in her ears and comforting warmth shuddered through her body.

“You are the most beautiful woman I have ever seen.”

Her body tingled with a newfound excitement that sent a delicious wave of pleasure through her. She wanted him more than ever before and longed for his touch. She'd been trying to do the right thing by staying away from Luca, but she couldn't stop herself from loving him. It was far too late for that. How was it possible, when in fact she had never stopped?

His hair tickled her skin as he lowered his head and allowed his lips and tongue to tease her left breast. Her nipple responded immediately under his skillful tongue, taut and throbbing. Thoughts of Miguel, Natalie, and dimmed lights were long gone from her mind as Luca continued to roll the bud between his lips and suck, lick, and gently nibble until stars filled her vision.

Heat burned between her legs as she clamped them together to hold on to the tingling sensation deep within her. She arched her back to bring herself closer to his mouth as he moved his attention to her other breast and offered it the same expert attention.

"Luca…" She breathed deeply and reached for him, weaving her fingers into his hair, needing to hold on to something before she fell into oblivion.

How could just his mouth alone make her feel like this? She was teetering on the edge of something new and intoxicating and didn't want to cross it. She had never known sex—known intimacy and love—to be like this. Luca and Daniella had decided together to wait until they were married, to tighten their unity and love for one another. Her only sexual experience with Miguel was akin to rape. However much it sickened her to admit to it, that was all it had been. Daniella had quickly learned that fighting Miguel wouldn't achieve anything but further pain. Now safe in Luca's secure and tender grasp, she couldn't believe they were brothers.

Luca moved down her body and continued to show undivided attention as he kissed his way over every inch. His hands traced over her ribcage, hips, and belly. Even though soft, his hands still possessed a roughness, a masculine strength. His hand rested on her thigh before he nudged them further apart to settle himself between of them.

"Oh, Luca…"

"Shhh," he whispered before he dipped his head and kissed the sensitive spot of her inner thigh, the pad of his thumb following his kisses in soft, circular movements against her skin.

His mouth found her sex, exploring and owning it with each lick. Gently for a few strokes, before he slipped his finger inside and slowly thrust in and out.

Oh, dear God.

The slick wetness of her desire was evident and

gave him easy access. Luca entered a second, stretching finger and skillfully moved both inside her. The cocktail of kisses to her highly sensitive bud and the curling of his fingers in a come-hither motion quickly sent wave after wave of pulsating pleasure throughout her core.

"Luca, please. I can't take any more." She called his name as she arched her back, trying to get closer to him.

She held the pillows beside her with one hand, and with the other she twisted through his hair, using the grip to pull him closer, deeper into her. His tongue swirled over her fully charged clitoris one last time before he rolled it gently between his masterful lips, bringing her closer to the edge of the same oblivion she had been nearing since entering his room.

"Yes, yes. Oh God, please don't stop!"

Luca teased for a few more moments. His fingers pumped faster inside of her, massaging her g-spot and clit, as his tongue worked untold miracles.

"Come for me, *querida*. Close your eyes and just free fall." He breathed against her skin. The breath on her hot, wet skin was too much. She cried out in ecstasy and reached for his shoulders with both hands to brace herself.

Wave after wave of euphoria engulfed her from

head to toe and washed over her. Floating so high, all Daniella could hear were thunderous beats pulsating in her ears in unison with the multiple waves of divine pleasure.

She rested the back of her forearm across her closed eyes and listened to her ragged panting. As she slowly drifted back, she tried to suck in a gulp of composure. Her body still tingled with remnants of pleasure. She never knew such passion, such connection, was possible. For the briefest of seconds, she wanted to cry with a happiness she'd never experienced before, but managed to hold back the emotional torrent.

"Are you okay?" Luca lifted her arm away from her face and gently placed it beside her.

Opening her eyes, she was greeted by his face close to hers. She hadn't felt him move from between her legs, it was as if time had vanished whilst she was composing herself.

"Yes." A breathless whisper was all she could muster in response to him.

Luca's mischievous grin was infectious and she couldn't stop herself from smiling back.

"Good. Think you can handle a round two?" He pushed a strand of hair aside and kissed her forehead.

"Mmm-hmm." She raised her head and pushed her lips against his. She could taste the saltiness of her release on his lips and tongue as his tongue swept in a swirling motion inside of her mouth.

Her heartbeat slowed and the blissful flood of pleasure slowly left her body as Luca's hard, throbbing erection pushed against her belly. For a fleeting second, she wondered how on earth he was going to fit inside her as she looked at his straining arousal. She reached down and took the long, thick shaft in her hands and longed for him to be deep within her. She could see the sheen of his pre-ejaculation and had a burning desire to taste him, something she had never wanted to do before. She'd never felt so alive, so exhilarated.

She placed one hand on his chest to push him away a little. "Wait."

"What's wrong?" His brow creased with worry.

She wanted to return the pleasure even though Luca had told her it wasn't necessary. She wanted to. She needed to.

She'd never been so awakened by a man before. The very thought of him inside of her mouth brought her near to the edge again.

She sat up and kneeled in front of him on the bed.

Taking him in her hands, she began to caress him with a slow and steady pace. A primitive growl left him as he reached for her and tried to pull her away.

"Daniella, you are playing with fire." His voice was stern and matter-of-fact, and warning flashed in his dark eyes.

I know exactly what I'm playing with.

She looked up at him once more before she took him into her mouth. She was reassured when he groaned and his eyes closed.

* * * *

Damn it!

Luca wasn't sure how much longer he could hold back before coming. He needed to be inside her before she had him finishing right there and then. He opened his eyes and took firm hold of her hips before pulling her on top of him.

Her eyes locked with his in silent agreement and she gently started to lower herself on to his rock hard girth, inch by inch, stretching herself to accommodate his straining masculinity.

Luca softly bucked his hips back and forth to help ease himself further inside of her. Daniella stifled a gasp as she bit down on her lip.

"Relax," he whispered, cupping her cheek and pulling her down to meet his lips.

With each thrust it became more comfortable and both moved together in sync, in natural harmony. Luca looked up. Her wet curls were bouncing with each rise and fall as his thrusts filled her completely. He was finally making love to her. After all these years, after all the heartache, he was finally inside of her, mentally and physically. She was his. She may have given her virginity to Miguel, but she was his now.

Luca moved her so that he was on top and shifted his weight on to his forearms. Daniella wrapped her legs around his body and pushed her mouth onto his lips. Her body trembled once again as she sunk her fingernails into his back and clung to him tightly. He withdrew to the tip before plunging back into her for the final time, a crescendo finally consuming the both of them. Luca rested his forehead against hers as they both attempted to control their breathing.

They made love several times throughout the night before Daniella fell asleep in his arms. At five in the morning, Luca was still wide awake with her curled up against his chest. Her lips were parted slightly and her curls, now dry, tumbled over her shoulders and breasts.

The silk bedsheet draped over the curve of her hip bone and bump, leaving her upper body exposed to the hot Rio air.

She was the definition of everything that was just in the world. His heart stung as though he had been stabbed with a steel blade over and over. He had no idea how he was going to tell her to leave in the morning.

Chapter 11

Luca hadn't slept all night. He'd stayed beside Daniella and watched her sleeping peacefully; she was blissfully unaware of his intentions. The knot in his stomach twisted tighter and tighter until he couldn't bear it anymore. He had to do something to distract himself from this mess he'd created. He carefully peeled her arm from across his chest and quietly made his way to the en suite, closing the door firmly behind him.

If only it could be so easy. He ground the heels of his hands into his eyes. *Shit. Shit. Shit.*

How could he possibly go through with kicking her out on to the street now, after last night, after everything? How the hell could he let her go?

How could he allow her to leave his life, again? And it would be his own doing. His plan of bittersweet revenge suddenly didn't seem as tempting as before.

Turning the shower faucet on to full, Luca stood under the cool stream and rested his palms on the tiles. The water cascaded over his shoulders and down his back. He hoped the water would wash away the memories of last night and soothe his confused thoughts.

What was happening to him? He was always in control, never second-guessing himself. He'd had his fun and knew it had been worth it, that he had accomplished something…hadn't he?

He'd expected satisfaction from the revenge he sought, but it eluded him. The ever-tightening knot in the pit of this stomach was beginning to weigh him down as guilt overtook him.

Be done with Brazil for good. Get a grip. Remember what she has done to you. She broke your heart, crushed you. She eloped with your brother for Christ's sake!

The words echoed through his thoughts and reminded him of what she had done so easily, so flippantly five years ago. She hadn't even looked back as she'd walked away from him into his brother's arms.

My brother of all people!

Daniella had turned her back on him and left him a broken man for a long time. Work had been his only saving grace, allowing him time, space, and a distraction he could throw his energy into. Eventually pent-up anger and the window of opportunity had led to his determination for precious revenge. She had to feel the same pain as he had.

She just had to.

Luca finished his shower, dressed in one of his Hugo Boss suits, and made his way to the kitchen to fix himself a black coffee. From today, business would return to normal and his life in New York would resume. He would sell his property in Rio and be done with Daniella once and for all. It was as clear as day and simple. It would all be over in the next couple of hours and then he could move on with his life. He would keep her under observation, and when the baby was born, he would assume custody and be the sole parent for the child—his brother's child. It was his family obligation, and the child would be better off with him.

The confusion in his mind cleared as he worked out each step.

Luca poured himself a third cup of coffee and carried it with him into the bedroom. Daniella hadn't moved an inch. The wicker chair opposite the four-poster bed offered him a place to stew over his thoughts as he gazed at her. Part of him wanted her to wake so he could get this over with. He also wished just as hard—if not more—that he didn't have to, that she could stay there with him, in their home forever as it should have been years ago.

God damn his thoughts, his emotions. He'd had them under control, but now they threatened to escape from where he had locked them away.

As if on cue, Daniella stretched out her arms to his side of the bed, reaching for him before her eyes flickered open. "Luca?" she muttered softly.

He didn't answer. He couldn't answer.

Daniella twisted to look at the clock on the wall before she turned to face him. The smile that spread across her lips when she saw him was like a punch to his stomach. Her hair was loose and fell softly across her shoulders. He thought back to a few hours ago when his hands had been entwined in her hair, gently pulling against it to gain access to her neck. Those spellbinding lips… His mind was wandering.

"There you are. What are you doing up? It's only six-thirty. Come back to—" She stopped mid-sentence and sat up in bed. "Why are you dressed for work? It's Sunday."

Luca inhaled deeply as he stood. He threw back the dregs of his coffee and turned his back to her. To look out of the window unseeingly was far easier than to look her in the eye.

The coward's way.

"What's wrong, Luca? You're scaring me."

This was it. This was farewell. The end.

Just get it over with.

"You need to leave."

"I'm sorry?" He heard her shuffle around in the bed, but he remained still and didn't look at her.

"I said you need to leave. Today. You can get yourself ready and then I want you out of my home."

"What…I don't understand? What's happened?" Her voice cracked with a nervous giggle.

Why did she have to ask questions? Why couldn't she just leave and make it easier for the both of them?

Luca rubbed his jaw as he gathered his thoughts. He could hear the soft *swish* of her body slipping across the silky sheets and prayed to God she wasn't moving nearer to him. He couldn't deal with her being in close proximity. She just needed to leave and then he could move on—life could be simple.

"Luca?" Her shaky voice came from directly behind him. "Have I done something wrong? I thought last night…"

Frustration began to build up inside of him, brewing and eating away at him.

"This just isn't working anymore," he lied, his gaze

fixed steadily on the rising sun.

It could work. Of course it could work, if you let go of the past.

A nervous laugh escaped Daniella's lips. "What isn't working? Last night wasn't—"

"Last night was part of my plan. You were just a toy to me and now I'm finished with you. You were nothing more than another notch on my bedpost." He turned on his heel. She stood mere inches from him. "Call it revenge if you wish."

Damn! Why did he turn around?

His eyes fell upon her, petite and vulnerable, confusion written on her face. The ivory bedsheets cocooned her and contrasted with her olive skin. He clenched and unclenched his fists, attempting to rid the imprint of her on his skin, from his memory.

A tense silence lingered in the air for a few moments whilst she gazed steadily at him.

Luca swallowed hard and ground his teeth together as he tried to hold together the mixture of emotions simmering inside.

"I see. Revenge?" she said in a matter-of-fact tone, but the rolling of her bottom lip between her teeth couldn't hide the telltale nerves he'd become accustomed to.

That was it? That was all she had to say? He'd expected more than three words from her at least.

Small tears formed at the corners of Daniella's eyes, but she blinked them back before they could fall. There was no going back. This was his plan, he'd waited so long for this sweet moment and he was going to see it through to the very end.

Hell, it isn't sweet, but I am seeing it to the end.

"All of this—the last four weeks, it's all been for nothing...just for vengeance?" Daniella frowned as she calmly spoke each word, her gaze not shifting from him.

Luca stuffed his hands into his trouser pockets and shrugged in a nonchalant fashion. "Simple as that."

She bit down on her lip and a light frown creased her forehead. "Revenge for what? Me leaving you and marrying Miguel?"

Damn it. That hurt.

"Naturally." Slowly he clapped his hands together three times to applaud her quick understanding.

She blinked and replied calmly. "You don't need to worry. I will be gone in ten minutes." Daniella held the sheet with a white-knuckled grasp as she turned her back and made for the doorway. "Miguel was right about you after all."

He barely heard her words as she reached for the door handle.

"What did you say?"

She twisted the knob and pulled the heavy oak door back on its hinges. "He hated you. He always said you were nothing but poison, and now I'm starting to believe it."

Daniella's words cut through him like a knife, twisting and turning deep inside of his chest. She didn't face him and kept her gaze fixed on the door handle.

He knew his brother wasn't his biggest fan, they'd never seen eye-to-eye, even as young children, but hate? Miguel had hated his own flesh and blood?

Times had been hard whilst they were growing up; both had craved further attention from their parents. When they had passed away, Luca had been the sole caregiver for Miguel and the pair had started to fall deeper into crime and gang life. By the age of fifteen, Luca led a local gang, with his young brother following in his footsteps.

He'd always noticed how much anger Miguel had inside him—it almost powered him through life. He'd thrived on fights and violence and often instigated it.

Luca knew he had failed his sibling and should have provided a better upbringing for him, but he had tried his hardest to keep him fed and as safe as possible. One positive aspect of the gang was that they looked out for their own.

Several years later, he'd extended his hand to help Miguel leave the Rocinha only to be hurled abuse and shunned. But none of this explained Miguel's bitter hatred for him. He couldn't believe that. As much as he disliked his brother at times, Luca couldn't hate him.

The only person Luca hated was standing in front of him. Daniella was the one who had caused this trouble. She had chosen to leave him and entice his brother. She had brought this all upon herself.

"I can't believe I wasted all these years loving you, and for what, your sick games?"

"You never loved me." He spat the words at her. It was true, how could she have loved him and then so easily have given him up. He gave her credit for her amateur dramatic skills—she was a believable liar.

Her footsteps faded as she paced down the hallway toward the guest room, leaving him standing alone.

* * * *

Daniella closed the guest bedroom door firmly

behind her and slumped against it for support. The bedroom, which had been hers for the last four weeks—her haven—was actually nothing more than Luca's guest room for his toy. She brought her hand to her mouth to stifle her cry as tears rolled down her cheeks. Her heart was shattering piece by piece like a fine crystal thrown to the ground. Why had he done such a cruel thing? She'd truly believed he still cared for her, genuinely cared for her and her baby, but it had all been a façade.

Everything had been a lie, a ploy and utterly fake.

Of course she could have stood and fought her case, poured her heart and the truth out to him, but it wasn't worth it. He'd made up his mind, had his fun and ended it. Nothing she had to say would change anything now.

She shook her head and realized she didn't know him at all. He wasn't the man she'd loved, the man who had rescued her and held her in his strong, safe arms. Daniella sucked in a deep breath and attempted to compose herself. She wasn't sure she could stand without the door's solid support, but forced herself to try. She had to get out of the house now. Right now.

Dropping the sheet, she let it gather around her ankles as she grabbed the freshly washed underwear that she had arrived in. She stepped into the briefs and hooked the brassiere as quick as she could with trembling hands. The dress she had worn on the day Luca had shown up, hung in the wardrobe, freshly washed and untouched since then. Daniella removed it from the hanger and pulled it over her head. She slipped on her old shoes and took her purse from the bedside dresser. She'd arrived at Luca's home with nothing but the clothes she'd stood in, and she was sure as hell going to leave the exact same way. She was not going to take a single item with her; everything he'd bought for her was part of his sick plan. It was tainted and worthless.

She slung her purse over her shoulder and opened the bedroom door. This was it. She would never see him again. Her head was chanting *good riddance*, but her heart ached. She thought it wasn't possible to hurt more than she had done five years ago, forced to watch Luca walk away from her as she'd stood obediently beside Miguel. She truly believed it was not possible to hurt beyond the agony she'd felt that day, but this topped that tenfold.

Her legs shook as she stepped out of the bedroom and closed the door behind her. The hallway appeared longer than ever and she wondered how she would make it to the end. It now seemed to symbolize a never-ending stretch, like a void into her unknown future. She placed her hand on her stomach and silently promised her baby things would be fine.

Luca was nowhere to be seen. The *click-clack* sound of her sandals as she descended the stairs echoed through the still mansion even though she tried to be quiet.

Luca appeared as she stepped off the last step and leaned against the dining room door frame with his arms folded across his chest. Inches from her, his masculine scent filled her nostrils for the last time.

She stood nervously fiddling with the clasp of her purse.

"Here's your key. Will you please say goodbye to Maria for me?" Daniella placed the silver house key into the center of his extended palm and watched as his long fingers enclosed around it.

He was calm and composed—and she could barely bring herself to look at his face. She desperately wanted to hate him, hate him more than anything, but instead her heart was just numb. Loosely focusing on the pinhole of his jacket she whispered, "Goodbye, Luca."

Daniella turned the handle and stepped out into Rio's sunlight. Her throat constricted as waves of panic washed over her—she was alone and had no idea where she was heading to, but she was adamant she would manage. She had no choice.

She had to, for her child's sake.

Chapter 12

Daniella had hailed a passing taxi after finding some change in her purse. She gave the driver the coins and stepped out of the hot vehicle as she looked around her and let a small sigh escape her lips. She was back to her old surroundings.

Back to square one.

She'd sworn never to return to the place she'd called home with Miguel, but right now there was no other choice. It was that or the streets, and this was the lesser of two evils. The streets could be a perilous place during daytime, let alone in the shadows of the night.

Daniella walked through the tangle of alleys and tried to stay under some of the canopies in an attempt to avoid the intense rays. Since the taxi ride, she was sick and exhausted; her heart was broken after all.

She stopped at a nearby street vendor and handed the correct change in exchange for a bottle of water. A violent combination of nausea and dizziness took over as she stumbled for the support of wall behind her. She sipped at the water and desperately hoped it would cure the unpleasant sick sensation but to no avail.

Nothing can cure a broken heart, you stupid girl. She stood, shoved the water bottle into her purse, and continued down the narrow street.

A few blocks deeper into the *favela* city, she stopped as a wetness trickled warmly between her thighs, quickly followed by an intense cramp in her lower belly. She rested her hands against the wall for support as she breathed through the sudden pain.

"No, no, no. Not yet."

She was going into premature labor.

* * * *

"Make sure the plane is ready. I'm leaving for New York within the hour."

Luca pocketed his cellphone and wallet and closed his laptop. It was time to return to New York. His business in Rio was finally finished and there was no further reason to stay there.

Although he'd treated Daniella as if she was a business matter, his usual satisfaction that came with a business win was missing. He had kept himself busy since she had left by attending to emails, phone calls, and various pieces of paperwork, in an effort to avoid his mind wandering. He expected to feel victorious, content, finally accomplishing his payback, yet inside he was numb and anger consumed him. Slipping the laptop into the carry case, he wished his emotions could be pocketed just as easily.

The cellphone vibrated against his thigh. *Incompetent staff!*

"Yes?"

"*Senhor* Venancio, please excuse me for contacting you out of the blue."

He removed the cell from his ear and checked the screen. Dr. Menezes's name and number flashed in front of him and instantly his gut twisted painfully as he raised the phone back to his ear.

"Doctor?"

"You must come quickly."

The snaking sensation in his stomach tightened further as he heard the urgency in the female doctor's voice. The baby. His mind raced with questions, was the baby okay? Was Daniella okay?

"It's Daniella, she is in labor."

"Labor, but she's…" Luca did a quick mental arithmetic. "She's four weeks early?"

"She's at the *posto de saude* emergency facility in Rocinha. She's contracting every ten minutes. You really do not have long if you want to witness the birth of this child, Mr. Venancio."

Luca ended the call and pocketed his cellphone for the second time within five minutes. He slumped into the leather office swivel chair and rubbed his eyes with his thumb and forefinger with such pressure it hurt.

He would not allow himself to be drawn into this; he'd finished with her. *Finished!* She'd made her bed with Miguel and now she could sleep in it. End of the story. He rested his head back, closed his eyes, and tried to forget the doctor's panicked voice now haunting his mind.

"Damn it!" He grabbed the arm of the chair.

Guilt crept up on him, he could almost sense it prowling through his veins and preying on his heart. He couldn't leave her in pain, alone in a decrepit hospital bed. He still had an obligation to the child and to Miguel. Even if Daniella's words were true and Miguel hated him, he had loved his younger brother, and now he knew he had to fight for his own flesh and blood.

His cell vibrated again with the doctor's name flashing across the screen. Twenty minutes had passed and he was sure the doctor would have expected him to be on his way. He held the cell to his ear and listened as Dr. Menezes explained that Daniella was experiencing some complications.

"I'm sure she could really do with your support as of now, Mr. Venancio."

A click sound filled his ear to signal the doctor had hung up on him.

He tapped the phone against his lips whilst he considered what to do. After a couple of minutes, he decided to swallow some of his pride and he grabbed a set of keys. His body shuddered with more guilt, what had he done to her? He'd put her and the child at risk, all for the sake of his own petty games.

Complications. The doctor's words resonated over in his mind.

What if— He pushed the sinister thought aside as he slid into his Aston Martin 1-77. It didn't even bear to think about the consequences he may have to face. Tearing down the driveway, a tornado of dust filled his review mirror as he slammed his foot down harder on the accelerator.

* * * *

Luca slammed on the brakes and the Aston Martin came to an abrupt stop outside the hospital. The wheels screeched and skidded against the dusty road. He was back, deep within the *favela*, and the sticky heat hit his face when he stepped out of the air-conditioned car. He climbed the steps two at a time toward the entrance that led into the stuffy lobby room. It was filled with people, coughing and spluttering, and some clutching at various wounds. He sensed their gaze fall upon him one by one as if summing him up for his inappropriate appearance. Not many people wore expensive suits to a public hospital facility in the heart of Rocinha.

"Daniella Venancio, I need to see her." He rested both hands on the small, wooden desk and caught his shaky breath. One small, circulating fan blew into his face and cooled his skin. The heat in the building was unbearable.

A middle-aged lady shrugged her shoulders and replied, "I'm sorry, you need to take a seat and someone will be with you shortly."

"But I need to see her now!"

Her unhelpful manner angered him, but his agitation came more from within. It was his behavior that had put Daniella there. Him. His actions. No one else. The undue stress he'd placed on her over the last four weeks, and especially the last twenty-four hours, had finally taken its toll on her.

The woman turned her back on him and shuffled

through a stack of papers.

Luca turned and headed toward the main corridor. He wasn't waiting around to be told when and where he could go. The receptionist called out after him, but he elbowed his way through the set of double doors.

The corridor was scattered with waiting patients sitting on plastic chairs and lying on stretchers. He cursed Daniella for coming there. Why hadn't she used the money in the account he'd set up for her weeks ago and admitted herself to the private clinic? He hadn't demanded the money back this morning, knowing full well she was going to need some financial support over the next few weeks until the child arrived. Although, he was sure she was probably unlikely to use it due to stubbornness.

Pushing through another door, Luca arrived in a room lined with many hospital beds and further stretchers squeezed around the sides. Some had curtains pulled tightly shut and some remained open. The noise was overwhelming and impacted on his ability to think. Clinical machines beeped methodically, women cried, and men swore as they were stitched up.

Madre de Dios!

He scanned the room but didn't see her.

"Argh!"

He turned to face the direction the scream had come from. It was Daniella.

He quickly moved toward the direction of her voice and pulled back the cotton material of the curtain.

"I can't do this, doctor. Please..." Daniella was lying on a simple hospital bed, propped up by a couple of pillows.

He looked down at her and his heart constricted. Her eyes were wide with fear and her cheeks stained with dried trails of tears. He had no doubt she was petrified and in excruciating pain.

"Finally!" Doctor Menezes took hold of his forearm, pulling him firmly into the small bay. "I thought you weren't going to make it."

Luca knew the doctor worked selflessly at the public hospital as a volunteer on days when she wasn't in her private rooms.

"What are you doing here?" Daniella cried. "Get out! I said get out!"

"It's okay. I called him, Daniella. You need to have somebody here with you," the doctor attempted to explain.

"I don't need anyone, especially not him... Argh!"

"Remember what I explained to you…deep breaths. That's it…nice and steady. You're doing wonderfully."

"I have a right to be here. You are bringing my family into this world. Why the hell didn't you go to the clinic?" Luca stepped closer to the bedside.

"You don't have any right. This baby isn't your family. He or she has nothing to do with you. Doctor, please make him leave. I don't want him near me."

"*Senhor* Venancio, I asked you here to help. Daniella is weak and still has a long way to go, please do not agitate my patient."

He sucked in a sharp breath and reached for her hand.

"She collapsed three blocks away. Street vendors brought her here. Her labor has happened very quickly…too quickly. She most likely had no time to think about what to do, let alone which hospital to attend," Doctor Menezes whispered into Luca's ear.

He cursed himself. The guilt finally captured his heart and devoured it with an aching pull.

"I said don't touch me… Oh God—"

She held tightly on to Luca's hand and crushed his fingers together.

"That's it, Daniella, breathe nice and slow…in

through the nose and out through the mouth. Wonderful." Dr. Menezes's voice was soothing and reassuring, even to Luca's ear.

"I don't want you here," she cried through the tears that rolled down her cheeks.

"I'm here for Miguel and the baby's sake, and you do need me right now."

"Miguel? Miguel deserves nothing from you. He hated you. He wanted you dead."

Luca looked at the IV drip and asked the doctor, "What medication have you got her on exactly?" His voice was stern. He did not like to hear his brother and family name slighted.

"It's just IV fluids. We cannot stock many strong painkillers here because of break-ins." The doctor frowned.

Luca attempted to process Daniella's words. *Hate. Dead.*

"You're in a lot of pain. You don't know what you are talking about. Please stop these ridiculous lies and save your energy."

She snatched her hand away from his grip and shook her head from side to side. "They're not lies."

Luca swallowed. A small part of him wanted to

hear what she had to say—to play at her own game. "Fine, tell me everything I need to know about my brother. Get it out of your system." He drew a nearby chair close to the bed.

"You wouldn't believe me." Her bottom lip trembled as she spoke.

"Try me."

"I just…wanted to keep…you safe…"

Daniella's incoherent ramblings didn't make sense to him.

"You're not making any sense. Why do you still insist on this ridiculous notion of my safety?"

"Because Miguel wanted to kill you. How can you love and honor a monster like that? Tell me."

He almost laughed at the outrageous accusation. "Why would my own brother want to kill me?"

She wiped her cheeks with the back of her hand before she answered. "Because he despised you, envied you. Jealousy made him evil. You had the good job, the nice things, the girl…you had bettered yourself and left the gang, and he didn't want to see you happy."

"Are you sure there is nothing else but fluids in that IV?" Luca asked the doctor.

"Positive."

He watched Daniella breathe through another contraction, and she squeezed his hand so tightly the bones in his fingers clicked.

"If what you're saying is true and he was so evil, why the hell did you marry him?"

"I had no choice."

Luca laughed. "So, he tied you down at the altar and forced the words from your mouth, did he? I can't believe I'm even listening to this and engaging with your deluded fantasy."

"He wanted to hurt you and knew the best way to do that was by using me. I had to hurt you. He knew how much you loved me, and he wanted to see you heartbroken…for something to finally go wrong with your perfect life."

"I still don't understand where my life comes into this? So what, you chose my brother, it didn't mean I would curl up and die of a broken heart."

Her bottom lip trembled uncontrollably. "He gave me an ultimatum. He said if I stayed with you, he wouldn't rest until he found you and killed you. Or I could simply end our relationship—break your heart by marrying him. Leave you and choose the better brother as he put it. Only then would he spare your life."

Luca stood up and rubbed the back of his neck. His disbelief began to waver. Surely she couldn't make up such implausible stories like this?

"What about the baby? You were not planning a family?" He shook his head in disbelief.

Neither of them spoke for several seconds.

Her face contorted and Luca was unable to determine whether it was due to his question or the contractions.

"I asked you if you were planning a family."

Daniella covered her face with her hands.

He pulled both her hands away from her face. "Answer me."

She struggled to whisper. "No."

The anguish in her expression tore at his heart. Was she really trying to say what he was thinking? *Surely not.*

"I don't understand. So the child was an accident? Not planned?"

"None of that matters now."

There was no doubt in his mind Daniella loved her baby, but she hadn't chosen this?

As if someone had flicked a switch in his brain, it all began to register slowly. Piece by piece the jigsaw puzzle became clearer—the bruises, the constant worrying, the apprehension and the nerves when he touched her. The revulsion for his brother evident every time she spoke of him. Had his brother taken her body against her will over the years, resulting in the situation she was in right now?

"He raped you?" Even the word disgusted him.

Daniella turned her head to face away from him.

"I think perhaps you may like to go and get a drink, Mr. Venancio?" The doctor shifted from foot to foot and looked anxiously at him.

"No, I'm fine." His gaze was intent on Daniella. "Tell me, Daniella." He took hold of her hand again, this time softly rubbing the pad of his thumb across her knuckles. "Please, just look at me. I'm not the monster you think I am."

The slightest nod of her head answered his demand.

"Jesus Christ," he whispered. "So…everything was against your will?"

"Yes. This child is lucky to be alive after the way he battered me black and blue on a regular basis."

"Why…why didn't you leave…just run? When I had left Brazil you must have known I would be safe."

He was used to dealing with hard negotiations and

world renowned business tycoons, not this. Not Daniella's emotions. Not his own emotions.

Not a child about to born any second!

"Miguel said if I left, he would find you wherever you had gone. I had no money, no family. I was practically brainwashed and I had no clue what to believe in the end."

He leaned forward and brought her hand to his lips, careful not to touch the IV.

"So you have lived a life of imprisonment, for me? You sacrificed your life for what…to save mine?"

Daniella simply nodded.

"Why?"

"Because I loved you. If that meant us being apart, then so be it. I was prepared for that. At least you were still alive in the world, breathing, and not on a mortuary slab."

He opened his mouth to respond, but words failed him. He wanted to gather her in his arms and hold her close. He'd been told the couple was in love, that his brother had won the girl fair and square, or so he had been led to believe. His private detective had not reported any observations apart from Daniella attending the hospital once in a while.

"Shit," he muttered to himself as another part of the puzzle clicked into place. "You said loved?" He looked down at her hand still in his.

"Yes. Loved."

"But—"

"Daniella, we're ready," the doctor interrupted. "You're fully dilated. A few really strong pushes and your little one will be with us."

"Please, just go."

The hard lump had returned at the back of his throat and however hard he swallowed, it wouldn't budge. Was this the physical manifestation of how guilt felt? He owed it to her to stay firmly by her side.

He kissed the back of her hand again. "I'm not going anywhere. You need me here, and more importantly, I want to be here."

"I don't want you seeing me like this."

"I'm not leaving you or this little one, do you hear me? You are beautiful. You are amazing, and you can do this." He placed his hand on her rock hard belly.

As the doctor shuffled past Luca, he lowered his voice and said, "The baby is premature, do you have facilities to care for such demands here?"

The doctor shook her head. "No, we don't. The

women here just pray that their child arrives into the world strong and healthy."

Luca dragged his free hand over his face. The faintest murmur of a prayer passed his lips for both mother and the child about to be born into the doctor's arms.

"Just one more big push, that's it. Daniella, your baby is here."

Daniella could hear Dr. Menezes's voice, but it seemed muffled, as if she was in another room and calling through the wall.

Tiredness washed over her and she could barely lift her head to look at baby.

"What…what is it?" she whispered, closing her eyes.

"You have a perfect…" Luca's voice faded further away into the same room as the doctor.

* * * *

"You gave us all a fright coming into the world so suddenly, little one."

Luca. He was close by. Slowly, she opened and closed her eyes a couple of times to adjust to the light. The room was different, but strangely familiar. The clinical whitewashed walls and terracotta curtains triggered a memory. The curtains. She was at the clinic where Luca had arranged for her scans.

"Daniella?" His hand was on top of hers.

"What...happened?" Her voice was croaky. She closed her eyes again. *How did I get here?*

She recalled hearing Luca's voice telling her that her baby had been born and then...nothing. The rest was a strange and heavy blur. She concentrated on the dimmed spotlights in the ceiling as the dizziness subsided. What happened?

Her baby!

"My baby! Where's my baby?"

Panic rushed through her veins and her heart banged furiously in her chest. The cold numbness of dread filled her entire body and paralyzed her for the faintest of seconds.

"She's right here." Luca smiled and his face was radiant, a brilliant white smile.

He held a small bundle completely swaddled in soft pink blankets. A tiny, perfectly shaped nose peeped out of the top of the material.

"Sh...she?" Her voice caved as tears burned the corners of her eyes. *I have a girl?* A painful lump formed in her throat as she swallowed.

"Yes. You have a beautiful and healthy daughter. Congratulations."

She put her weight on to her palms and pushed herself up the bed, desperate to get a look at her baby. The pink blankets were neatly wrapped around her daughter as she peacefully slept in Luca's arms.

To see him hold her baby—her daughter—just inches away, and to have the potential to get up and leave frightened her. Judging by what he had put her through, she knew he was no better than his brother. The only difference was Luca's financial stability, which meant he had immediate access to ways and means of ensuring she never saw her flesh and blood again. Her stomach somersaulted and nausea washed over her.

"Please, can I…" Daniella stretched out her arms. Fear clawed at her throat and stopped her midsentence. She'd never wanted anything more than to have her child in her arms right now.

Was he going to snatch her away? She recalled him stating he had obligations to the child when he'd first shown up in Rio. Did he intend to fight for guardianship?

Luca's brow furrowed as he gazed down the infant. He gave the bundle a gentle squeeze and placed a kiss on her forehead, and she stirred in his arms.

"Of course."

Hesitant, Daniella watched as he stood and loomed over her. The maternity ward blankets and their contents appeared so teeny between his muscular arms. For a moment, Luca could have been mistaken for the doting new father who was learning how to handle his newborn child—all fingers and thumbs.

"Here." He gently placed the child into Daniella's waiting arms.

The churning in her stomach stopped as she held her baby close to her body for the first time. Unconditional love coursed through her and she knew right then that she would do anything for her. Absolutely anything. She would go to whatever lengths were necessary to protect this little one, anywhere and anyhow.

"My beautiful little girl." She dipped her head closer and whispered to the sleeping newborn. "I'm your *mamãe*."

Forgetting Luca was present, she focused her undivided attention on the miracle in her arms and traced a finger down her daughter's cheek, stroking the downy hairs that covered her small, rosy cheeks. She was completely oblivious to the chaos she had caused just hours before. Her small, rosebud-shaped lips were slightly parted as she breathed, her chest rising and falling with each minute movement.

She wriggled in her mother's arms before she opened her eyes. Large, dark brown pools greeted Daniella before her eyelids crept down and sleep claimed her again.

Luca leaned forward and smiled again. It was genuine and full of adoration. She'd never seen him so animated, so alive with love. It was amazing how a newborn child could make a person feel. However harsh a man could be, however nasty and full of angst and betrayal, a tiny newborn baby could bring him to his knees.

"She looks just like you." He caressed the child's soft cheek with the back of his index and middle finger.

Concentrating on the little girl's face as she nuzzled close to Luca's fingers, Daniella couldn't see her resemblance at all. Instead, she had all the features of the Venancio bloodline, with the chocolate brown eyes and a head of thick black locks. There was no disputing her family name whatsoever.

"Can you please leave now?" She hesitated and

drew her gaze from her child's to his.

She'd whispered the words and now wished she'd voiced them louder, with confidence and control, but she feared if she angered him he would be impulsive with his actions. He was a Venancio after all and nothing would surprise her now.

He was silent and unmoving for a moment before stuffing his hands into his pocket.

"*Sim.*"

Daniella's heart leapt. The way he looked at her baby was mesmerizing, as if the little girl had him spellbound. He kissed his forefinger and rested it on her cheek.

Please don't kiss me.

She closed her eyes and silenced the war between her heart and her mind. More than anything she wanted his lips on hers, his arms locked around her and her baby. They could be the perfect family. *No. No, we can't be the perfect family. Far from it.* She reluctantly opened her eyes.

"I'll be outside."

She paused before she spoke, searching for the right words. "I would rather you left…completely."

She watched the sleeping child, nestled safely in her

arms, and purposely avoided any further eye contact with Luca. The soft click of the door handle told her that he'd left.

Chapter 13

The doctor appeared in the doorway seconds after Luca left.

"You're awake." She smiled. "And I see you have finally been introduced to your daughter."

Daniella returned the smile. "She's perfect. No…she is beyond perfect."

"She certainly is. You did brilliantly." The doctor placed the blood pressure cuff around Daniella's arm and positioned the SATS monitor over her index finger. "Do you have a name for this little one yet?"

"No. I thought I still had time to think about it."

"Well, life is full of surprises. There's no rush, you will think of a beautiful name for her when you least expect it."

Silence hung in the air as the doctor recorded Daniella's observations, the blood pressure cuff creating a *whoosh* sound as it released and beeped with the result.

"What happened? I remember hearing her cry, but…I can't seem to recall anything else."

Doctor Menezes folded up the cuff and hung the stethoscope around her neck as a flicker of a frown crossed her face.

"After your baby was born you suffered a postpartum hemorrhage and lost an extremely large amount of blood." Standing still, the doctor looked from the sleeping child to Daniella. "It was touch and go. If you'd have stayed at in Rocinha…" She swallowed and held Daniella's gaze. "Well, let us just be thankful that Mr. Venancio was able to get you here quickly. Ambulances do not venture into the *favela*, and even if they did, the wait would have been too long. Yes, we provided you with the care here, but it was he who managed to drive you here in time and ultimately save your life."

Tears stung the corners of Daniella's eyes as realization hit her front on. She would never have seen her daughter if it hadn't been for Luca. She looked down at the contented child.

"And she's okay?"

"She's absolutely fine. A few weeks early, but the neonatal nurses and the consultant have checked her over and there is no need for any special care. She just needs lots of love and nurturing."

Daniella nodded, unable to speak for fear of unleashing the torrent of emotion inside of her.

"He didn't leave your side, you know. From the minute he arrived in Rocinha until just this very second, Mr. Venancio has been right beside you with this little one."

* * * *

Daniella concentrated on her daughter who had dozed off after nursing for the countless time. Not that she minded. Daniella loved holding her small miracle of life close as she nuzzled skin-to-skin.

A tray of freshly prepared dinner had been served just minutes before and Daniella's tummy rumbled. Picking up the solid silver knife and fork, she took a mouthful of the beef *churrasco* and coconut lime rice that the hospital chef had prepared on request.

"Anything you wish to eat, our chefs will prepare it. You name it," the nurses had told her.

It was delicious and she quickly appreciated how hungry she was as the food hit her belly with comforting warmth.

A knock on the door startled her and her fork clattered against the fine china plate. Before she could call out for the visitor to enter, the door handle turned and she was met with Luca once again.

He'd left a few hours ago when she had insisted and

she should have known it was too good to be true to believe he would actually follow her wishes completely.

"May I come in?" He stood in the doorway and waited for her answer.

She pushed the tray away from her lap and attempted to shuffle toward the edge of the bed.

"No, stay where you are. You are meant to be resting."

"What do you want?" She tried to keep her voice down.

"I would like to come in and talk to you instead of hanging around the doorway."

"Fine, but be quiet."

Luca stepped into the room and quickly closed the door behind him. He held a Louis Vuitton travel bag in one hand and a huge spray of tropical flowers in the other. "I brought you some of your things. Figured you would want a change of clothes, some toiletries—"

"They aren't my things. You purchased them."

"What am I going to do with a room full of perfumes and women's clothes? They're for you."

"Throw them away. Give them away. Sell them. I don't care what you do."

He tilted his head to the side. "Please, just keep

them."

His dark, expressive eyes almost pleaded with her. She hesitated before she nodded in agreement and pulled her robe more tightly around her.

"These are for you." The cellophane crunched annoyingly as he placed the neatly wrapped bouquet on the table.

"You do realize flowers won't fix everything?" The brusqueness of her words even sent a shiver through her body.

"That wasn't the intention. I just thought you might like them."

She cast her gaze over the ridiculously huge bunch of flowers and admitted they were exquisite. An explosion of color from the *laelias*, *poppy-papaver* and *quesnelia testudo* flowers reminded her of Luca's stunning private garden and she wondered if they were from there. The sweet perfume filled the room and created a tranquil, heavenly atmosphere.

"I wasn't sure what you would need, so I asked Maria to pack three of everything." He lowered his voice.

"Thank you," she whispered before catching her trembling bottom lip between her teeth.

"It's only some clothes and personal necessities. Please, I haven't come to upset you." He moved closer and hovered at the end of the bed.

He had showered and changed clothes, and was cleanly shaved with the scent of fresh cologne filling her nostrils. Jeans teamed with a loose white cotton shirt, the first two buttons undone, revealed his signature dark curls scattered across his chest. She tried to blink and tug herself away from him, but that ever-powerful magnetic force had taken hold over her once again.

"No, I mean…thank you for saving my life. Again." She stumbled over her words.

He shoved his hands into his jean pockets and shrugged. "There's no need to thank me."

"I want to…need to. It doesn't feel right not to."

He shrugged again and scuffed at the floor. "Well, there really is no need. Besides, it makes us even now, I guess."

"No, it's two-one to you actually."

"Hey, who's counting?" A faint grin crossed his mouth. The light nod of his head told her that he accepted her gratitude.

Heat rose in her cheeks as his gaze lingered on her. This was ludicrous, she reminded herself of how he'd treated her less than forty-eight hours ago.

Sensing his stare leave her, she looked slowly up to see him watching her daughter.

"How is she?" He took a couple of steps closer to the small crib.

"She's fine, a real sleepyhead." Her heart pounded so loudly she was sure he could hear it.

Was he there to take her daughter? Was that why he was being so civilized—to distract her?

"Have you chosen a name?"

Daniella nodded. "Yes. I'm going to name her Lara, after Doctor Menezes."

He kneeled down on his haunches and reached for the child's tiny fingers, which instinctively closed around his large digit.

"Just perfection. It suits her. Little Lara."

The sincerity in his tone tugged at her heart.

"You should be very proud," he said.

"I am."

The intense look in his hooded eyes was back on her. "And how are you feeling?"

She fiddled with the robe tie. "I feel fine."

That's a lie. I'm beyond exhausted. I'm sore and aching in places I never knew I had. And my heart feels as if a train has hit it.

“Your ability to lie has clearly weakened over the years.”

Daniella dropped the robe tie in her lap and straightened her posture. “Why are you really here? You’ve done what you needed to do.” She nodded toward the overnight case. “You can leave now.”

“We need to talk.”

“What else could you possibly want to talk about? Why won’t you leave us alone?”

Luca moved closer to the head of the bed, each step taken with hesitation and not the usual self-assurance she was used to seeing.

“There is nothing left to talk about. Nothing.” Her heart pounded in her chest, her throat, her head; the sound was deafening as emotion flooded through her. She loved Luca, but hated him. She worshipped him, but despised him. She needed him, but wanted rid of him. She wanted him as the father for her baby, but wanted him nowhere near her.

“Everything you said yesterday, it was all true?”

“Why would I lie?”

Luca’s stare fixed on hers, his dark eyes bored through to her soul, to reach deep within her for the truth. He tucked his index finger under her chin and rested his thumb on her cheek.

Closing her eyes, her shoulders fell as the confidence that had held her steady since his arrival swiftly left her.

"I am so sorry, Daniella. If I had known—"

"You would have done what?" Daniella leaned slightly into the palm that now cupped her face.

"I would have protected you. I would have fought for you." He cupped the other side of her face with his free hand.

"You couldn't have fought for me when you were dead."

"I could have tried."

"I truly believed it wasn't possible. I couldn't have had you killed right in front of me. I had to let you go, even if it meant breaking both of our hearts." She opened her eyes, aware of the familiar stinging sensation at the corners. "I was always yours and nobody else's. Every single day I was just yours, in here." She peeled his hand from her flushed cheek and placed it above her galloping heart.

Luca rested his forehead against hers. "Nothing I will ever say or do will prove just how sorry I am for all of this. I will spend the rest of my life showing you how truly sorry I am for my brother's cruel, twisted mind. I'm sorry for…for…" He glanced at the innocent child caught in their turmoil and shook his head. "Most of all, I am sorry for how I treated you. It was unconceivable. There is no excuse for it." His fingers moved to the back of her neck and wove between her curls. His grip on her tightened as he spoke. "I wanted to hurt you as I thought you had done so easily to me. My stupid, childish mind. I thought you didn't love me anymore. I don't expect you to understand me nor forgive me, but I ask of you…I beg of you to please try. Please let me be a part of yours and my niece's life."

Daniella bit down on her lip, not quite sure how to respond. Part of her wanted to leave Rio and him behind. Things couldn't be the same as before. *Could they?*

Yet another part of her wanted him more than anything. Her heart wanted him more than she'd ever wanted anybody. She had always loved just him from the very second he had caught her in the street.

"Luca, I–" She looked from him to the crib.

Words failed her, could she really forgive him for his actions? Truly forgive him?

He reached into his jean pocket and a retrieved a

small, neat square box. "This is far from the most perfect of timings and a long way from Sugarloaf and champagne, but I have to fight for you this time around. I cannot lose you again."

Is he really about to do what I think?

She watched cautiously as he looked toward the crib. "Daniella, I don't want to be her distant relative, a vague memory as she grows up." Luca looked back at her, his eyes ablaze. "And I don't want you to be a distant memory either. You are the most amazing thing to ever happen to me. I love you."

I love you. How could those three words offer the illusion of safety and warmth and yet so flippantly that of dishonesty and lies? Only Luca could manage that.

He knelt down on one knee and took hold of her trembling hand. "I promise to love you, honor you, and worship you with every inch of my being. I promise to protect you and never allow anyone to cause you pain, most of all me."

As if in slow motion, he pulled back the top of the sleek black box to reveal the familiar patterned platinum band, iced with a square polished diamond. It looked just the way she'd remembered it over five years ago.

"That's…it's impossible," she muttered as she ran

her fingertips over the ring.

The band was firmly tucked between the velvet material that held it in position, but Daniella was able to catch a glimpse of the words engraved on the inside.

Always thankful for faulty bags and runaway oranges. All my love. L.

It was definitely the ring. The same ring. Her ring.

"Is that the ring? My…my ring?"

"Yes."

"But how? Where did you get…"

She'd been made to pawn it only days after she had left Luca and thought she would never see it again. How Luca now held it in his very hand was beyond her.

"It doesn't matter how." He softly kissed each of her knuckles. "No more games. No more lies. No more wasting our lives."

Daniella covered her face with her palms as hot tears streamed down her cheeks and through the gaps between her fingers. He gently pulled her hands away from her face and held her gaze.

"Will you do me the honor of marrying me?"

She couldn't contain the cry that finally escaped her lips and quickly turned into ragged sobs.

Leaning forward, he whispered into her ear. "Will

you be my wife?”

There he was. Her Luca. The honest, sincere, and magnificent man she had met all those years ago. It was really him. No lies or charades in tow, just him wanting her.

“Yes!”

Luca took the ring from its box and carefully slid it on to Daniella’s finger.

She reached for his shirt collar and pulled him close with such fervor that it hurt as her lips pushed hard against his.

All of the hurt, the anger, and the unconditional love had amounted to this moment in time and neither was ever letting go again.

They were finally together as if they had never been apart.

About Samantha Darling

I live in Essex, not too far from London, with my identical twin boys and two Bedlington Terriers. We're crammed into our rather cozy two-up two-down terrace and we can barely swing a cat, but hey, we love it. I work part-time as a nurse, but when I'm off duty, you will find me either chasing the kids around like a headless chicken, head buried in a book, or tapping away at my stories.

I have always loved to read and romance is by far my favorite genre! You can easily escape into such promising worlds, where sexy Alpha males lead the way and strong heroines often can't help but fall head over heels in love. I adore a Happy Ever After, as I'm sure we all do if we're honest, right?

Reading and writing go hand in hand, and from the day I could read, I enjoyed writing. To put pen to paper and conjure up weird and wonderful little stories was what I thrived on. English was my favorite class at school right throughout to secondary, and I will always be thankful for the teachers who gave me the opportunities to develop and be creative. If I remember rightly, one of my first stories was called *The Turkey Who Could Talk*…but I'll tell you more about that some other day!

Samantha's Website:
www.samanthadarlingromance.com
Reader eMail:
Samanthadarling1986@hotmail.com

CPSIA information can be obtained
at www.ICGtesting.com
Printed in the USA
FFOW04n1119200116
20608FF